# Deadly Evidence

DINO DE LAURENTIIS Presents an ULI EDEL Film

MADONNA   WILLEM DAFOE

JOE MANTEGNA  ANNE ARCHER  "BODY OF EVIDENCE"

JULIANNE MOORE And JURGEN PROCHNOW

Line Producer MEL DELLAR  Music By GRAEME REVELL

Film Editor THOM NOBLE  Production Designer VICTORIA PAUL

Director Of Photography DOUG MILSOME B.S.C.

Co-Producers BERND EICHINGER And HERMAN WEIGEL

Executive Producers STEPHEN DEUTSCH And MELINDA JASON

Written By BRAD MIRMAN  Produced By DINO DE LAURENTIIS

Directed By ULI EDEL

NOT BASED ON THE NOVEL BY PATRICIA CORNWELL

# Deadly Evidence

A novelization by Harrison Arnston
based on the script by Brad Mirman

An original storyline not associated with
Patricia Cornwell's novel *Body of Evidence*

## HarperPaperbacks

*A Division of HarperCollinsPublishers*

This is a work of fiction. The characters, incidents, and
dialogues are products of the author's imagination and are not
to be construed as real. Any resemblance to actual events or
persons, living or dead, is entirely coincidental.

HarperPaperbacks    *A Division of* HarperCollins*Publishers*
                    10 East 53rd Street, New York, N.Y. 10022

Copyright © 1993 by HarperCollins*Publishers*
All rights reserved. No part of this book may be used or
reproduced in any manner whatsoever without written
permission of the publisher, except in the case of brief
quotations embodied in critical articles and reviews. For
information address HarperCollins*Publishers*,
10 East 53rd Street, New York, N.Y. 10022.

Cover and insert photography courtesy of Dino De
Laurentiis Communications

First HarperPaperbacks printing: February 1993

Printed in the United States of America

HarperPaperbacks and colophon are trademarks of
HarperCollins*Publishers*

❖ 10 9 8 7 6 5 4 3 2 1

◆Andrew Marsh was flat on his back, his slightly hooded eyes open wide, glazed with excitement and ecstasy. He was breathing heavily, his arms extending back from his shoulders, his restrained body bucking wildly. He tried futilely to lift his head from the satin-sheathed pillow, then let it fall back.

He moaned.

He was sixty-three, but looked younger; a robust man with an athletic build and handsome face, a face that displayed a full range of expressions from stinging pain to indescribable pleasure—all in a matter of seconds.

The source of both the pain and pleasure was the woman straddling him. She was half his age, dazzlingly beautiful, with classic features and a magnificently sculpted muscular body, a body topped by blond hair cascaded in a series of waves and curls to just above her shoulders. Her voluptuous high breasts jiggled provocatively as she straddled her lover, her hips grinding into his pelvis and her bare buttocks smacking loudly against his legs.

Suddenly she slapped his thigh hard, eliciting another moan from the older man. Then she slapped his other thigh, the blow much more powerful, the force of it leaving a red impression on Marsh's chalky-white skin.

Again, he moaned, utterly lost in the strangely harmonious confluence of pleasure and pain.

She closed her eyes, threw her head back, and thrust her breasts forward, then ground her hips into him as she fondled her breasts and pinched her taut nipples. Slowly her head came forward and her long-lashed eyes opened wide. A wide smile exposed her bright and perfect white teeth.

It was obvious that she was rapturously enthralled, not only with the act of sex, but with being in complete control of everything that was taking place. She was setting the pace, controlling the activity, determining who did what to whom. And she reveled in it.

Marsh moaned again, then noisily sucked in another mouthful of precious air.

The woman leaned forward, one nipple gently brushing his lips, then the other. As his head rose again from the pillow she quickly raised her body, moving her tantalizing breasts just out of reach. Marsh whimpered like a child.

Now she was sitting straight up, rocking again, harder this time, her head turning from side to side as she steadily increased the tempo. Both lovers were bathed in sweat, and their skin seemed to glow in the subdued light emanating from the bedside lamps.

The rocking continued, the sound of skin slapping skin reverberating throughout the large bedroom, a sound interspersed with moans of pleasure from both lovers. Marsh grunted, then gasped, each breath accentuated with a guttural cry. The woman responded by reaching down and gripping his hips, jerking them upward demandingly, forcing him deeper inside her.

He issued a long, low wail that seemed to build as the woman increased the pace another notch.

"Unbelievable." Detective Jack Reese shook his head in amazement and turned from the television set to look at the man lying on the bed. It was the same man in the very same bed. Only now the woman was gone and the man was dead, his eyes wide open and his mouth slack-jawed.

The bed was surrounded by men with rubber gloves on their hands; crime-scene technicians, probing, checking, photographing, making notes. The usual.

Dr. McCurdy, the county medical examiner, watched as two of the technicians lifted Marsh from the bed and placed him in a body bag already resting on a gurney. The lifeless eyes of Andrew Marsh were still wide open, staring at nothing. The doctor leaned over the body, took a final look, then zipped the bag closed.

"I think he was faking it myself," Detective Reese said, a smile tugging at his lips as he opened the bedroom door and watched the gurney being wheeled out of the room.

Dr. McCurdy ignored the remark, but the remaining technicians laughed. Then they returned to the task at hand, a task made more difficult by the presence of the still-running videotape. The sounds of passion continued to echo through the high-ceilinged room.

The bedroom revealed much about Andrew Marsh. Spacious and well appointed, with a large walnut four-poster bed dominating the room, the central focal point. Expensive coverings graced the walls and heavy silken drapes covered the windows. Thick carpets covered all the floors. One large oil painting, a nude mounted in a gold-leaf frame, covered a portion of one wall, while two smaller nudes were prominently displayed on another. All three were originals by Peter Paul Rubens.

The message was clear. The room reeked of money—and sex.

Reese was a hard-nosed, experienced detective. His lived-in face reflected that background, and though Portland wasn't as bad as some cities, there were enough killings to make any cop jaded. He'd seen it all, or at least he thought he had until this morning. This one was unique.

Griffin, Reese's partner, with just a few years less on the job, was still watching the tape. "There's worse ways to go," he said.

"You mean come."

One of the forensics technicians laughed. "Gives a whole new meaning to the state nickname, doesn't it?"

Another asked, "What the hell's that?"

"You don't know?" The technician laughed. "Oregon's the Beaver State."

The man who'd asked groaned.

Reese pressed a button on the VCR and

the tape started rewinding. As the tape sped on, the two lovers looked weird with their jerky motions in reverse, making no sense this way. Almost comical. It made Reese laugh.

This case was different, all right. For evidence, there were just some sexual toys and a video of two people screwing each other's brains out. Now one of them was the dead man, and if the dead man had been a truck driver instead of one of Portland's wealthiest men, they probably wouldn't be there at all.

The street was cluttered with official vehicles by the time Assistant District Attorney Robert Garrett arrived at the scene. Several police cars, the ME's van, and an unmarked detective's car sat in the unrelenting rain.

Garrett grabbed his battered black umbrella, opened it, and stepped out of his car into the rain. A single uniformed policeman guarded the door of the stately home.

He peered down the street as a news truck pulled away from the curb, then fishtailed on the wet street, its tires failing to find traction on the slick pavement.

It had been raining for hours. Already

the storm drains were flooded and water rushed down the gutter like a small creek. Garrett leaped over it and landed on the curb. Then he began to hum a few bars of "Singing in the Rain" as he walked toward the house. Already he was girding himself, just like the homicide detectives and the technicians. They all did it.

He stopped to let the men with the gurney wheel past him and load the corpse into the ME's van. Dr. McCurdy was right behind them.

"Lousy morning for it," Garrett said, moving his umbrella over McCurdy to afford some protection.

"Mr. Andrew Marsh, tagged and bagged," McCurdy said. "Better him than us, huh?"

"So what did him in?" Garrett asked as he watched McCurdy climb inside the van.

"Looks like cardiac arrest."

"Really?"

Dr. McCurdy grinned. "You look disappointed. Who knows, maybe I'm wrong. I'll call you later."

Garrett nodded, then walked quickly toward the house. In truth, he was disappointed, for this was the kind of high-profile case he loved—if in fact there *was* a case. But there had to be *something* or they wouldn't have called him in.

In his midthirties, Garrett was of average height and trim, except for some slight puffiness in his cheeks. The trimness was due to regular workouts in his home gym. His swept-back black hair topped a face that was round and pleasant, with thick eyebrows, dark, often twinkling eyes, but eyes that could become cold and foreboding in an instant. His full, wide lips were often formed in a smile, but he was a man of moods. Sometimes the smile became a sneer.

He was a vain man, acutely aware of his good looks, not entirely narcissistic, but close, and near-obsessive about his wardrobe. He liked to dress well and look good, and everyone knew it. But his almost overpowering charm, the result of street smarts and education, overshadowed his vanity, and made him more human.

The overall effect—the carefully manufactured persona—had an impact on women and juries, and Garrett knew it. That confidence was expressed in every move he made. Everyone liked him, especially women, for he had an uncanny knack for being able to read them, a skill he exploited to the fullest.

At the front door Garrett closed his

umbrella and handed it to a uniformed policeman. "Full house," he said, offhandedly as he sauntered into the large foyer.

"I'm not a fucking doorman," the cop said, glaring at Garrett's back for a moment. When he received no reply, he dropped the umbrella in a corner of the hall.

The interior of the house was impressive. Garrett let out a low whistle as he took it all in. Andrew Marsh had been one of Portland's wealthiest men, and his eclectic taste was clear in the furnishings, very classic, from the thick carpets covering the floors to the costly originals on the walls. The entire house bespoke a man who liked to spend his money, not hoard it.

Here and there, carved wooden pedestals held busts of ancient Greeks and Romans, while others displayed more modern works, some of them by American sculptors.

There was an understated elegance about the place that made Garrett wonder if Marsh had hired a decorator or chosen everything himself. Probably a decorator, he thought. Most businessmen had the tastes of a wild goat.

Garrett took a minute to fix the image of the rooms in his mind, then headed upstairs, passing a departing cop on the way. As he wandered down the darkened hallway he could hear voices in the bedroom, a soft murmur as the crime team went about their business. He also heard another sound, the low, throaty moan of a man, then the more intense, sharper cry of a woman in ecstasy.

His curiosity piqued, he pushed open the door of the bedroom, instinctively stuffing his hands in his pockets so he didn't inadvertently touch anything.

Though the body was gone, the bedroom was still crowded with crime-scene technicians. Garrett knew most of them and nodded hello.

His attention was immediately drawn to the walnut-framed thirty-inch television set, the source for the sounds of passion he'd heard earlier.

A man he immediately recognized as the deceased was lying on his back. Atop him was a beautiful blond woman, both people lost in the throes of passion, their sweating bodies moving in unison, the woman arching her back, her hands caressing her breasts, her fingers kneading her nipples. She bent forward over the man, licking his face, then moved away teasingly.

The man struggled to match the woman's energy level. He was wide-eyed and panting, and it was hard to tell if he was enjoying himself or in some kind of pain. Garrett guessed it was pain.

"Nice quality," Garrett said, impressed with the video equipment. He wasn't much of a voyeur, preferring to have sex instead of watching someone else. Pornography usually bored him to tears.

"Nice ass!" one of the technicians countered.

Detective Reese stood beside Garrett, peered at the tape, and grinned. "That was the tape in the VCR, and the power was still on when we got here."

One of the technicians asked, "You need a pair of gloves, Bob?"

"Yeah, thanks."

Garrett snapped on the elastic gloves. "So the sucker had a heart attack watching his home movies. What do you need me for?"

"He was tied up," Reese said.

Garrett turned toward the bed then smiled. That was more like it.

"Okay," he said. "Tell me more."

Reese snickered. "I've heard of remote, but—"

Now Griffin joined them. "He had some beautiful rope burns on his wrists."

One of the technicians kneeling by the

nightstand held up a small braided leather whip and an enema bag, made a face, then placed them into an evidence bag. He then picked up a silver metal object and stared at it curiously. It was circular in shape, actually a circle within a circle, with a small bolt sticking from one side, looking much like a small screw vise.

"Anybody know what this is?" the technician asked.

While the others looked at it Garrett answered, "It's a nipple clamp."

The technician stared at him. "What?"

"A nipple clamp," Garrett repeated.

The technician laughed. "How do *you* know that?"

"He's from L.A.," Reese said by way of explanation, laughing himself.

Garrett shrugged. "I just happen to be a well-informed person."

At that, the whole room exploded in laughter. The technician turned the clamp every which way, trying to figure out how it worked. Finally he asked.

"Who cares? Just bag it."

The technician bagged it. "Kinky shit," he groused.

Garrett turned back to Griffin. "Marsh had rope burns on his wrists?"

"Yeah. I'd say he was into S and M. I've

watched that tape five times. It sure looks that way."

Garrett looked at the tape more closely. Griffin was right. Marsh's eyes seemed to be fearful as he struggled. The camera angle was such that Marsh's hands could not be seen. Just his face and most of his body. Perhaps his hands had been tied to the bed.

Garrett suppressed a grunt of disgust. He'd never understood the attraction sado-masochism held for some people. To him, there was great pleasure in sex, and pain played no part in it—pain and pleasure were opposites, not partners.

The camera captured the woman's face in glimpses, only when she'd turn and appear to look at the lens, aware that she was being photographed. She was some-thing, for sure, and for a moment Garrett wondered what it would be like—

He turned away from the television set and watched as the technicians continued vacuuming, dusting, even using a small hand-held laser to bring up fingerprints invisible to the naked eye.

While he waited for the area to be checked he absorbed the sumptuous ambi-ence of the bedroom. As on the floor below, the furnishings were expensive and luxuri-ous. Again, the man's good taste was readily apparent, in the drapery fabric colors, the choice of wall-covering pattern, even the oils on the walls.

Once the area surrounding the bed had been checked, he moved to the bed. He examined the creamy-white satin sheets, the pillows, the bed frame, the thick posts rising high above the mattress, and even the mattress. His attention was drawn to the bedposts. He ran his still-gloved fingers over them, then motioned to the photographer.

"Harry, you want to get a picture of these gouges for me, please?"

The photographer came forward. "Where?"

Garrett pointed to the bed frame. "There, on the wood."

Harry peered at the marks, then started to arrange his lights. "Looks like she had him chewing on the wood."

Garrett shook his head. "Those weren't rope burns on his wrists," he said in a loud voice. "She had him handcuffed."

The room fell silent as everyone strained to see the scarred bedposts. "I thought only chicks liked that shit," Griffin said.

Garrett grinned. "Maybe she fucked him to death. Remember Rockefeller?"

There was no answer. The detectives

and technicians were still digesting Garrett's earlier comment about the handcuffs. Now things fell into place. Marsh had been handcuffed to the bed, unable to move. That's why his hands weren't visible on the videotape. He was just lying there, almost helpless, bucking and jerking while the woman slowly worked him over, using her body as a weapon. Until—

Maybe she *had* fucked him to death.

Garrett turned to Reese. "Who found the body?"

"His secretary came to pick up some papers this morning. Helluva shock. You want to talk to her?"

"She won't leave," Griffin added. "She thinks we're going to steal the silver."

"I don't blame her," Garrett said, grinning.

Reese looked past him and nodded. Garrett turned. A woman stood in the doorway. She was looking at the television set, her jaw firmly set, her eyes red-rimmed with grief.

"Do you want me to identify her?" she said, her voice filled with bitterness. "That's Rebecca Carlson."

Griffin, taking his cue from an embarrassed Garrett, who was giving the television set a sharp look, moved to the VCR and pushed some buttons, trying to turn it off. He finally found the right one and the image disappeared.

Reese leaned toward Garrett and whispered in his ear. "Rebecca Carlson is Marsh's girlfriend. And they had a date last night, according to Miss Braslow here. Miss Joanne Braslow."

Then he turned to the woman and said, "This is Bob Garrett. He's with the district attorney's office."

The woman stared at Garrett pointedly. He nodded.

She was attractive, with rich brown hair and a nicely shaped face that featured high cheekbones and pleasing eyes, though at the moment she was crying.

Reese continued to explain. "Miss Braslow was Mr. Marsh's secretary for the last six years."

"She found the body?"

"Right."

"She *killed* him!" the woman suddenly exclaimed. Then, tears streaming down her face, she left the room.

Reese turned to Garrett, his face wreathed in a big smile. "You got your first witness."

Garrett followed Joanne Braslow out to the balcony. The rain was gentle now, the sound of it hitting the roof a soft rush.

Joanne was staring off into space, her eyes pinched in anger, her hands gripping the railing so tightly her knuckles were white. She was pretty enough, but her makeup was subdued, like the clothes she wore. He guessed she was rather prim and inhibited, disgusted by what she'd seen her boss doing with the blond.

"What makes you think it wasn't a natural death?" Garrett asked, his voice soft and soothing, the natural charm oozing out of him.

She didn't look at him. "The whole situation was unnatural!" she said. "You saw her."

He waited. She turned to face him.

"No," he said. "All I saw was a videotape."

She spoke through tightly clenched teeth. "What you see is what you get."

Garrett took a deep breath, exhaled, then said, "I'm not a psychic, Miss Braslow. If you have something to tell me, I wish you'd—"

"He was sixty-three years old," she exclaimed. "He couldn't handle it. She wore him out, is that clear enough?"

He concentrated on her eyes, eyes that held contempt. Clearly she had nothing to contribute except her personal animosity toward the woman in the video. Not much of a witness after all.

"Well," he said, "I appreciate your analysis of the situation."

She was unimpressed. "Even if you don't call that murder, it was."

And then she brushed past him and went back inside.

He stood there for a minute, thinking. So far it didn't look much like murder. Fun and games, more likely. Except Reese had said the tape was in the VCR when they'd arrived. And it looked like Marsh had been handcuffed to the bed at one time. Was he alone when he died? Or was the woman in the tape still there? If so, why had the woman left without calling for help? And why had she left the tape in the machine?

As always in these cases, there were a lot of questions needing answers.

◆Frank Dulaney listened to the verdict being read, then patted his client on the shoulder and walked to the jury box to shake the hand of each and every juror, sincerely expressing his deep appreciation.

When he returned to the defense table, his emotional client reached out and embraced him warmly, unabashedly displaying his gratitude.

The man was small and older than Frank, but he had the strength of Atlas and the breath of a camel. Frank, feeling awkward, patted the man on the back, then looked over his client's shoulder and saw his courtroom adversary, Assistant DA Robert Garrett, fighting hard to hide his disappointment at losing a case. Garrett was eyeing Frank venomously. Frank simply shrugged.

They were in a courtroom that looked

like a thousand other courtrooms in a thousand other cities. Utilitarian, sterile, deliberately neutral, a place where the evidence was heard and justice meted out to those who had been found guilty of violating the law.

A room furnished with plain wooden tables for both the prosecutor and defense attorney. Another table for the clerk of the court. Behind them, unadorned wooden chairs, and behind a polished wooden railing that separated those involved in the criminal justice system from relatives, friends, and spectators, more wood, shaped in the form of benches.

A jury box with fourteen stiff, wooden chairs that could induce severe pain in a juror's lower back over the course of a prolonged trial occupied the far right corner.

A slightly raised bench dominated the front of the high-ceiling room, flanked by the Stars and Stripes and the flag of the great state of Oregon.

Everywhere, a profusion of smells—disinfectant, cologne, perfume, furniture polish—and the stale sweat of someone facing a jail term, or worse.

As the jury and spectators filed noisily out of the courthouse, Garrett pushed back his chair angrily, the sound of it scraping across the marble floor and echoing in the near-empty room. He slammed some files into his briefcase and snapped it shut, his face flushed, his eyes still blazing with undisguised anger.

Dulaney smiled inwardly, mumbled some words to his client, and sent him on his way. Then he, too, started putting files back in his briefcase.

Garrett was a respected prosecutor, and Dulaney was often his adversary, one of Portland's best criminal lawyers. They were about the same age, both outgoing, friendly, and accessible, but from there the personalities diverged.

Garrett was fastidious about his appearance, always dressing sharply. Frank figured it was because the man had once been poor and wanted to remind himself daily that he was poor no longer.

While Frank didn't flinch when he looked in the mirror each morning, he didn't have Garrett's natural charm. Frank was more rugged, his face square, with a large jaw and wide lips. His resonant voice was about an octave lower than Garrett's, and his brooding eyes often brought admiring glances from women. Not the kind of lustful glances Garrett received, but glances nonetheless.

While Garrett prosecuted and Dulaney defended, they were both professionals in the best sense of the word. Outside the courtroom, when they discussed a case, their meetings were frank and courteous, and more often than not the two men were able to reach some kind of agreement—a plea bargain—negating the need for a costly trial.

But they *were* adversaries, and both men were keenly aware of it. They fought to win, for winning was important. Inside the courtroom, each brought to bear every ounce of intelligence and experience, giving no quarter, and there were times when the competition between them seemed more important than the actual case.

In this case, Dulaney had eschewed the plea-bargain offer and had taken it all the way—and he had won. He could see that Garrett was stung by the verdict. While Frank felt a modicum of empathy for his adversary, winning gave him a deep sense of satisfaction. Winning was always better than losing, no matter what was involved.

The courtroom was now empty, save for the two lawyers. Together, they walked down the aisle.

Garrett turned and faced his antagonist, a

wry smile on his lips. "You got lucky, Frank."

He said it matter-of-factly, without a trace of resentment, but Frank knew he was still burning inside. It would pass.

Frank laughed. "You can't take it personally, Bob."

"I don't," Garrett said. "All I said was you got lucky."

Frank smiled and said, "If that was luck, I'll take it."

Garrett gave him a look. "Don't you miss working for the right side?"

Once they'd worked together as prosecutors. Then Frank, weary of the bureaucratic and political bullshit, had quit being a prosecutor and hung out his own shingle. The first few years had been tough, but when he kept winning cases, the word spread quickly. Now he was making more money than he'd ever made in his life.

And enjoying it.

Frank put on a straight face. It was difficult. "Bobby," he said, "the jury just said this *was* the right side."

Garrett nodded. "The pay sure is better."

Frank grinned at him. "Yeah, but I don't have the entertainment factor. I don't get to watch movies all morning."

He watched Garrett try, and fail, to suppress a smile. There were few secrets within the law enforcement community in the "City of Roses," the affectionate sobriquet given the city of Portland.

"Oh, you heard about that," Garrett said.

"Yeah. I'll wait for the bootleg copy."

Garrett turned serious. "It won't be making the rounds," he said firmly.

"The janitors'll have seen it by Wednesday," Frank retorted.

As the courtroom doors slapped at their backs Garrett said, "We'll see," then walked away, his hurried footsteps punctuating his parting remark.

Back at his office, a cheer went up as Frank entered the foyer. The office was large, expansive and modern, with large windows overlooking the river.

As Garrett had said, being a criminal defense attorney *did* pay better, and the office reflected this fact, from the luxuriously lush carpets and subtle wall coverings to the ceiling-mounted suspended light fixtures. There wasn't a fluorescent light anywhere in the office.

The furniture, even the secretarial stuff, was of high quality, as was the office equipment, all top-of-the-line. Not ostentatious, but solid.

On either side of a wide, carpeted hallway, cubicles housed associates, secretaries, one paralegal, two clerks, and one full-time investigator. The sound of fingers dancing across computer keyboards melded with the gentle whir of copying machines and muted ringing telephones.

The place seemed alive, vibrant, a busy, successful law office, and that's the way Frank liked it. It was good to let people know he was thriving, for success bred success. Even the perception of success was a plus.

One of the associates, Gabe Weider, Frank's junior partner, was ecstatic about the verdict, still bubbling over with enthusiasm.

"I heard you had the jury back in less than an hour," he said, his eyes expressing awe. Frank was his idol, his mentor, the man he most wanted to emulate.

"Forty-three minutes, actually," Frank said.

From a cubicle on the other side of the room, Charlie Biggs, the firm's investigator, yelled, "A new office record."

Biggs had a telephone pressed to his ear, but his massive black hand covered the mouthpiece. Frank grinned at him. Yes, it was a new office record, a resounding win.

Frank raised a victorious fist and went into his office, more cheers ringing in his ears.

His office was spacious, a corner suite with a view of both the river and half the city. He dumped his briefcase on one of the visitors' chairs, removed his overcoat, and hung it in the closet.

His personal secretary, a brisk woman in her fifties, calmly placed a list of phone messages on his desk. "Congratulations," she said coolly.

He was used to her composed deportment. She was never one of his cheerleaders, but it wasn't personal. If she failed to exhibit fervor for a cherished victory, he knew it didn't mean she wasn't on his side.

She was.

"Thanks," he said, hanging up his suit jacket and loosening his tie. "Anything special?"

She pointed to the list. "As a matter of fact, there is. The second name from the bottom, Rebecca Carlson? That's Andrew Marsh's girlfriend."

Biggs was off the phone and standing by the open door. Now he stuck his head in and said, "She's the chick on the tape."

Frank looked up at him in awe. "How do you know that?"

Biggs shrugged, feigning nonchalance. "From one of the janitors at city hall."

Frank threw back his head and laughed. Garrett would be purple with rage if he'd heard that.

"Really? They saw it?"

Biggs nodded. "I hear they had 'em a real dog-and-pony show going on up there. I'll tell you, sometimes white people just puzzle me. I mean, did this old guy really think he could keep up with a sweet little number like that?"

Frank took a seat behind his desk and leaned forward. "From what I hear, he did all right for a while."

Biggs shook his head. "I'm sorry, man, but I ain't never heard of no brother dying from too much pussy."

Frank glanced at his secretary. So did Biggs. Her face was red and her lips were so tight they were white. Biggs let out a laugh and clapped her on the back. She was not amused. Frank tried to smooth it out.

"They taught him to talk like that at NYU," he said.

She was not mollified.

Frank changed the subject. "What'd she have to say?"

"Who?" she asked.

"Miss Carlson."

"Oh. She asked if you could come to the funeral today, in case there was a problem."

"What problem?"

"She already thinks she needs a lawyer," Biggs said.

Frank grinned. "I love a client who's prepared. What's the word? Is there some reason charges might be filed?"

Biggs nodded. "Rumor has it that Garrett's fixin' to make something out of it. It's not as simple as it looks."

"I see," Frank said.

"I told her you were in court," Frank's secretary said.

"When is it?"

"It started at two."

Frank looked at the wall clock. Like everyone else, he'd heard the rumors about Rebecca Carlson and the death of Andrew Marsh. Now he was intensely curious.

It was already three. "I can make it," he said, standing up, rebuttoning his shirt and reaching for his jacket and coat.

"I hope there was a long eulogy," Biggs called after him as he strode out the door.

Dulaney turned and smirked at him.

◆　◆　◆

The cemetery was a fifteen-mile drive from the office. Frank reached it in less than twenty minutes.

He drove through the open wrought-iron gate and spotted a large crowd gathered in the western corner. He hoped it was the Marsh group.

Under leaden skies, the muted granite stones seemed somewhat forlorn, many in this older section showing the ravages of time and the violence of modern polluted air. The stones cluttered the sweep of green grass and carefully positioned trees, some of them fronted by green baskets filled with garish assortments of grotesque-looking plastic flowers.

Other resting places were more ostentatious; elaborate, ornamented mausoleums, the names of the dead chiseled in large Gothic letters in arches poised above heavy oak doors, virtually useless tributes designed only to assuage the living.

By the time Frank reached the site of the Marsh burial, the television crews were packing their gear into vans parked on a lane leading from the western section of the expansive cemetery. They'd gotten the tape they needed for the evening news broadcast, but the burial ceremony was continuing, a fittingly extended tribute to a man as well known as Marsh.

Marsh was often mentioned in the newspaper society columns. He was usually photographed wearing a tuxedo and handing a check to the head honcho of some worthy cause. His personal life was chaotic, but the papers played that down, protecting the man's image as best they could.

His death brought out Portland's best.

Near the site, a long line of freshly washed and polished parked cars—many of them stretch limousines—waited, uniformed chauffeurs sitting patiently behind steering wheels. By the grave itself, a large crowd of mourners huddled together in the sometimes biting breeze as they listened to the mumbled words of a minister.

This was the Marsh funeral all right.

Frank was forced to park a hundred yards away. He got out and sprinted through the forest of tombstones, then strode purposefully toward the gathering. As he neared the site his eyes took in everything, his ears picking up the sound of the minister intoning some final words, his voice carried by the breeze, ebbing and flowing.

He finally reached the rear of the throng and raised his head to better see what was going on.

The casket was being lowered into the

ground, the hoist creaking noisily. Some mourners threw single-stemmed flowers after it while others held handkerchiefs to their eyes and noses, weeping quietly.

Still others were stoic, their faces expressionless, their eyes dry. All were dressed in muted tones, grays and blacks, some wearing overcoats, while the more hardy simply braved the elements.

Frank took it all in, searching for a face he'd seen only on the television news.

He saw a woman, her face distorted by grief, her eyes swollen by tears, her gaze fixed upon someone standing directly across the open grave. He located the object of her attention. Another woman stood stiffly, dressed in an elegantly cut black dress, her soft blond hair moving in the breeze, her head lowered, seemingly unaware of the other's intense scrutiny. Frank couldn't see her face.

Frank turned to a man standing next to him. "Which one's Rebecca Carlson?"

The man gave him a look, then pointed to the blond.

As he'd suspected.

The service was over. The mourners turned to leave, several of them stopping to offer condolences to the obviously distraught woman with the hate-filled stare.

No one talked to the blond. The crowd eventually drifted off, leaving the blond alone with her thoughts.

Frank started to walk toward her. She wiped her eyes with a white handkerchief, then turned and immediately noticed Frank.

Her beauty hit him like an open hand. She literally took his breath away.

She was perfect. No other word described her. Her eyes, her skin, her nose, her lips, an assortment of delicacies miraculously arranged on one exceptional face. And from what he'd heard, there was a remarkable body underneath the fine dress. Those who'd seen the infamous tape called her a sexual machine.

Once totally uninterested, Frank was seized by the urge to see it.

Looking at her now, in this most solemn environment, Frank found himself suddenly and curiously tongue-tied, for there was more than beauty to this woman. There was something behind her eyes that seemed to penetrate his very soul, as if he was standing there naked, his entire being open for inspection.

"Miss Carlson," he stammered, "I'm sorry I'm late. I'm—"

She finished the sentence for him. "Frank Dulaney."

"Frank Dulaney," he repeated. "Do I look that much like a lawyer?"

There was bitterness in her response. "Who else would speak to me?" she said, her voice riveting, the tone strong and sure.

"His friends think I shouldn't even *be* here," she added quickly.

Frank, completely taken aback by her appearance, realized he was gawking at her. He looked away in embarrassment, taking notice of the stares they were getting from the other departing mourners, who were now climbing into cars, doors slamming, engines firing up, tires crunching against the rough asphalt.

By the time he returned his attention to Rebecca, she was moving away from him, toward the cemetery chapel, an imposing stone structure, its marvelous stained-glass windows shining brightly in the gathering gloom like a string of multicolored beacons.

He took some quick strides and caught up with her. She walked with purpose, her head held high, her chest pushed out defiantly, her eyes staring straight ahead.

"His friends aren't the problem," he said.

She stopped, turned, and looked directly into his eyes. He found her intense gaze surprisingly disconcerting.

"Will you represent me?" she asked.

Just like that. All business. She certainly didn't beat around the bush.

"There haven't been any charges filed against you," he said.

"But there will be," she told him. "You know that. Do *you* think I killed him?"

Her directness was off-putting.

"It's not something I ever ask a client," he told her. "All that counts is whether or not the DA can *prove* you killed him . . . beyond a reasonable doubt."

But there had to be something causing the DA to consider bringing charges, if that's what was happening. He wondered what it was that made her think charges were going to be brought.

"I loved Andrew, Mr. Dulaney," she said, looking up at him.

"You don't have to convince me," he told her.

"Why is it so hard to believe?"

Why indeed. People tended to think in simplistic terms when it came to sensational stories hyped beyond reason. They eliminated the gray areas and made decisions purely on preconceived biases.

She was young, beautiful, and sexually adventurous. That much was common knowledge, thanks to the leaks in the police department.

Andrew Marsh had been thirty years older than she, a respected businessman and philanthropist. Most important, he'd been rich. Conclusion? She was after his money. Why else would she spend time with the man? It was simple. That's what everyone thought.

He took a moment to answer. There was no use avoiding the truth. If he was to be her lawyer, she needed to know what was being said, the walls that had to be breached. "You know why," he said. "You're young, you're beautiful, and you were involved with a wealthy, older man."

"He wasn't old to me," she said softly.

"Then I'm sorry I said it."

And he was. Immediately.

She sighed. "I just buried a big part of my life, Mr. Dulaney. You should respect that."

Suddenly he felt ashamed. When first he'd seen her face, he was immediately aware of her sexuality. It was practically oozing from every pore of her flawless skin. There was an aura surrounding her, an unseen neon sign that spelled it out.

He'd reacted to it just as everyone else had, seeing only the obvious. He realized he was judging her from rumor and innuendo. While he hadn't seen the infamous tape, he'd heard enough about it. He'd envisioned it, in fact. And he'd made a judgment about this woman without ever having talked to her. Just like the rest of them. He knew better than that.

She was looking at him again. He felt that odd sensation growing stronger, an almost magnetic attraction that made no sense.

"You're right," he said softly.

"I *didn't* kill him," she said firmly.

He wanted so much to believe her.

3

◆"I don't understand," Frank said defensively. "I've defended killers, dope dealers, the scum of the earth. That's my job, and until now you've accepted it. But here, with a woman who has yet to be charged with a crime, you're throwing darts at me. What's the big deal?"

"No big deal," his wife, Sharon, told him. "It's just that you're going to be made to look the fool for taking this one for a client. I just know it. And I hate to see you lose."

He was baffled. "What on earth makes you say something like that?" he asked.

"She didn't love him," Sharon said assuredly.

Frank's face fell. "How the hell do you know?"

She looked at him and groaned. "What, you believed her?"

"Actually, yeah, I did."

"You're a romantic."

He looked hurt. "Not at all. I just know bullshit when I hear it, and this wasn't bullshit."

Sharon's eyebrows arched. "Really?"

"Really," he parroted. "How can you say she didn't love him without having met either one of them?"

"He was too old," Michael chimed in.

Frank glared at his son while Sharon smiled a triumphant smile. "Exactly."

He turned away and stared out the window of the café, a fabulously, deliriously successful enterprise owned by Sharon; a café and bookstore, the favorite hangout for Portland's hipper population, and unlike most "in" places catering to an often fickle clientele, this one had endured.

Famous authors on a book promotion tour made it a point to come by and autograph copies of their latest; sometimes they did readings. Either way, the café was becoming a must for authors, both local and national.

One wall was exposed brick decorated with prints and some signed art created by patrons. Soft track lighting cast a warm glow on the assembled art. The delicious aroma of fine coffee and good food permeated the room, adding to the warmth.

But books and good food were only part of the café's appeal. The bulk of its customers were not book aficionados, but were more interested in seeing and being seen wherever their peers chose to gather, and for the past few years this was the place to do it.

The place was almost always filled with conversation-minded people who often had to raise their voices to be heard. They prattled on about their work, their love lives, their hopes and dreams, compared notes, argued politics, religion, and sexual mores. Constantly.

Outside, there were almost as many as were inside, all waiting patiently for a cherished place at the bar, or better yet, a table. Some sat on the stylish French park benches while others milled about, standing, talking, occasionally peering in the window and wondering how long it would be before they could enter.

Frank had a table. He was privileged, the husband of the owner and manager. Sharon was a brilliant and hardworking entrepreneur, a great wife, and a terrific mother to their ten-year-old son, Michael, a kid somewhat mature before his time.

It was a good marriage, but subject to

the usual strains associated with making a living, pressures exacerbated by competing egos.

Frank and Sharon had managed to adjust to the wacky work schedule that conspired to keep them apart much of the time. Sharon usually started at six in the evening and stayed until closing time, two in the morning. She was still asleep when Frank awoke and prepared for *his* workday.

They shared the duties relating to Michael. And because there was so much one-on-one time with either of his parents, Michael, already precocious, was growing up much too fast to suit his father.

Frank figured the kid got his brains from his mother and his moxie from his father, but he was more a small adult than a young kid.

Sharon shrugged off Frank's uneasiness as meaningless. Michael was doing well in school, had many friends, was well behaved and rarely ill. How, she would ask, is a ten-year-old with an IQ of 140 supposed to act?

Sharon was a pretty woman, with copper-colored hair and intense eyes, whose taste ran to vintage clothing and velvet hats, both of which seemed not to be an affectation, but something as natural as a T-shirt and jeans on someone else.

In fact, the clothes suited her. They showcased her effervescence, the obvious enchantment with life that set her apart from some other women. She glowed. Constantly. She had drive and ambition, and being the sole owner of a business she'd inherited and made wildly successful served only to increase her energy level.

At the moment she was sipping coffee, leaning forward as she engaged in deep conversation with her husband, a man who was now representing the suddenly notorious Rebecca Carlson. And she wasn't happy.

Rebecca's face had been plastered all over the television broadcasts during the evening news, the lurid details connecting her with the recently deceased Albert Marsh topic A throughout the entire city.

Sharon had been idly watching the six o'clock news on the television above the bar while rinsing glasses. Her attention had been drawn at the mention of Albert Marsh's sudden death.

She knew the man, had met him twice. Both times he'd been a guest in the coffeehouse, and each time he had been there with a different woman.

He'd never been with Rebecca Carlson,

though, the woman now linked to his death. They'd shown her picture on television, and one look had convinced Sharon that she didn't like the woman.

And when she learned during dinner that Frank had taken Rebecca Carlson as a client, the news annoyed her. For the last few minutes she'd been trying to explain to Frank exactly why she was annoyed. It wasn't working, for he wasn't really listening to her argument. As usual, his mind was made up.

Frank glared at his wife. "That's a very narrow view of love," he said.

Sharon was not to be placated. "It's what the jury's going to think," she said.

Frank was about to reply, but one of Sharon's regular customers, a man, walked past their table and squeezed her shoulder. She looked up and beamed at him.

"Hi, Mark."

The man waved and joined a woman sitting at the bar. He leaned over and kissed the woman on the lips. Frank stared at him, upset at the man's familiarity with his wife. In fact, they were all just a little too friendly with her to suit him.

Sharon knew them all by their first names. It was one reason the place was so successful. Oh, sure, there was an ambience not found in most places, an atmosphere carefully crafted by Sharon, who had what amounted to a gift for decorating. But it was the force of her personality that made everything click.

Each night, hundreds of young people came and went, Portland's finest and most affluent young people, most of them on the fast track, their careers burgeoning, their lives full, each one known personally to Sharon Dulaney, who made it a point to memorize each name and every face.

She loved them all and they felt that warmth. She loved them not just because they were customers, but because they were her people. The movers and shakers, the intelligent, witty thinkers, the future of the city and beyond.

And they loved her right back. She made them feel important and appreciated. At other places, they were *just* customers. Here, they were all VIPs, and Sharon made a fuss over each one, inquiring as to their latest triumphs, commiserating with them if things had taken a temporary turn for the worse.

"Did he have any family?" Sharon asked suddenly.

Frank's mouth was full of food. He was still staring at the man and woman at the bar for no particular reason. He returned his gaze to Sharon and shook his head. Then, swallowing, he said, "Lots of wives, no kids."

A waitress approached the table and, after a nod from Sharon, whispered something in her ear. Sharon pushed back her chair and stood. "The register needs me again," she said. "I made a mistake going electronic. Are you here for a while?"

It was always like that at the café. The business came first, and he resented it. He didn't like playing second fiddle to anyone or anything, but Sharon was forcing him to do it.

"I don't want to hog the table," he said, looking around the crowded room. His voice was edged with sulkiness. He wanted her to urge him to stay.

She disappointed him. She gave him a shrug, as if to say she agreed with him. Then, as she saw another customer approach, she stood up, placed her hand on her hip, and pretending to be upset, said, "Jamie, how'd you sneak past me?"

The man laughed. "I saw some friends."

Sharon followed his gaze. "Those are your friends? Those are *my* friends."

She grabbed the arm of a passing waitress. "Pour a glass on the house for everyone at table seven."

Suddenly weary and realizing he was about to become irritable, Frank announced, "We're going to go on home."

"I have to lock up tonight," she said as she leaned over and kissed the top of his head.

He saw it as a condescending move. "Why don't you just hire a manager?" he muttered.

"Because at least I won't be stealing from myself."

It was her pat answer, and it was no answer. She always claimed she was indispensable, but he knew better. He knew lots of successful people who'd mastered the art of prudently delegating responsibility.

Not Sharon. She was a strong-willed woman, eager to have things her own way, uninterested in the mundaneness of motherhood and wifely posturing. This was her domain. Here, she called the shots and made all the decisions. The customers were eager to be *her* friend, not Frank's. This was her success, and Frank knew she wouldn't subjugate her feelings of triumph to cater to his less important needs.

It seemed her needs were filled by strangers.

His face expressed his growing annoyance. "Last time this week, okay?"

She pointedly ignored the comment. Instead she squatted down next to Michael. "Quick kiss, sweetie—"

She showered her son's face with kisses, then glanced around. "It's okay," she chided. "No one noticed."

Michael giggled. Sharon gave him a little wave good-bye, then walked toward the cash register, greeting customers, exchanging banter, at home in her element. Frank stared after her, as always somewhat in awe of her talent, but smoldering with resentment inside.

"Can you really screw someone to death?" Michael asked out of the blue.

Frank whirled and looked at his son. He was often stunned by such comments, which came frequently from the mouth of his son. They seemed so totally out of place from a boy so young.

He fought back the urge to reprimand the kid and forced a smile to his lips. "You don't have to worry yet."

Michael made a clucking sound with his tongue.

"Well, do you?" Frank said, teasing, his smile widening.

Michael was flattered, thinking that his father was asking whether he'd yet had sex. He hadn't, but he'd certainly heard a lot about it. He wondered what the excitement was all about.

"No," he said.

Frank opened his billfold and extracted some bills for the waitress's tip. Then he gathered up his and Michael's things. "You don't have to worry," he said.

"Worry about what?"

"About finding girlfriends. You're a good-looking guy."

Michael stared at his father. The grin was gone. Now his father's face was very serious. Michael took it to mean his father was telling him the truth, not teasing like before. His small chest swelled with pride.

"Let's go," Frank said.

The two got up from the table and walked toward the door, Michael feeling very grown up and Frank very tired.

As they reached the door Frank saw Bob Garrett enter the room, an exotic-looking brunette clutching his arm. Frank could almost hear the eyeballs clicking in the crowded room.

Most of the customers dressed casually, but Garrett was wearing an Armani suit, a European cut that emphasized his muscular body. His heavily starched white shirt almost glowed, the gold cuff links at his wrists gleaming brightly. He was a walking ad from *Gentlemen's Quarterly*.

His companion, her flowing dark hair hanging with precise carelessness over her shoulders, wore a low-cut red jersey dress that almost screamed for attention. Her full breasts rose and fell with her breathing, and her dark eyes surveyed the room with an intensity that captured everyone's attention.

She was wearing Moschino, Frank's favorite perfume. He'd given Sharon a bottle of it for her birthday. She'd worn it once to please him, but that was all. She preferred more flowery scents.

To the women in the room, Garrett's companion was a man-eater. To the men, she was a living, breathing fantasy. The rumble of conversation diminished appreciably.

Garrett, aware of the approving stares, had his familiar cockiness back. As Frank expected, the loss in court had been forgotten. There were other mountains to climb, and the woman on his arm looked like Garrett's first order of business.

Garrett made a point of not introducing her to Frank.

"Early night, Frank?" he chided.

"It's a real luxury, isn't it?" Frank said, smiling, looking at the woman, giving her a sympathetic nod of the head. She looked at him vacantly.

Frank wanted no more banter. He was tired from the mental exertion of the day. He wanted to be home relaxing, able to spend some time with his son, away from this crowd of overachievers.

Quickly he placed his hands on Michael's shoulders and pushed him through the crowd and out the door, the sound of soft laughter, tinkling crystal, and busy silverware fading behind him.

Frank saw Garrett again the next morning—Garrett and two homicide detectives named Reese and Griffin.

At Garrett's request, Frank and Rebecca appeared at police headquarters for what was termed "an informal discussion of the events surrounding the death of Andrew Marsh."

It wasn't informal and it sure wasn't a discussion. More like an inquisition. Two hard-eyed detectives and an all-business assistant DA; three people with a common goal—to tear his client apart verbally.

The interview room was tawdry looking and barren, as were all the police interrogation rooms. The rooms were designed to intimidate, to make the guilty think that further protestations of innocence would be futile. Sometimes the atmosphere alone was enough to cause the inexperienced and unrepresented to roll over quietly.

Dirty exterior windows allowed entry to pale yellow light. The walls were painted a glossy institutional green, and the amber-colored wooden table and chairs were marred by years of abuse. One wall was glass, a crisscross pattern of wires embedded within the windows. The windows overlooked the main corridor, which led to the small offices used by a cramped army of detectives.

Frank and Rebecca sat on one side of the table, closest to the door, while Garrett, Reese, and Griffin sat on the opposite side, their faces intent.

The three of them took turns asking questions, eyeing Rebecca hungrily, like lions after a weakened antelope. Now it was Reese's turn again, and the detective was relentless.

"A neighbor saw you go into Mr. Marsh's house at eight-thirty," he said.

Frank cut off the answer. "She's not denying she was there."

Reese ignored him. "Did you have sex with him?"

Another redundant question. Of course she had had sex with him, and Reese knew it. Half the city of Portland had probably seen the goddamn tape of Rebecca having sex with Andrew Marsh.

Rebecca answered with one word. "Yes."

Garrett asked, "Did you handcuff him to the bed?"

Again, Frank tried to stop her from answering. "Don't tell me it's relevant, Bobby."

Rebecca answered anyway. "Yes."

Frank glared at her. "You didn't have to answer that," he said, some heat in his voice.

"No," Garrett said, waving Frank off. "We appreciate her honesty and cooperation."

Sure they did. Frank was beginning to seethe. He'd warned Rebecca to let him guide her through this, and she was ignoring him. He felt as if he was losing control of the situation, and he didn't like it.

He'd told her before the meeting not to volunteer anything. Just answer the questions. Don't try to be cute. Don't insult anyone, and always wait before answering in case Frank wanted her not to reply.

Now, under the pressure, some of his instructions were being ignored.

"Bullshit," he snapped.

"What time did you leave his house?" Griffin asked, ignoring Frank's outburst.

Rebecca looked at Frank. He almost sighed with relief. He gave her a look that said it was okay to answer this particular question.

"Around midnight, I suppose." But then she added, "If I'd known it was going to matter, I'd have paid more attention."

Frank squeezed her elbow, giving her the signal to stop talking. She turned to Frank, her eyes filled with sadness, and said, "What's wrong with saying that? It's true."

"Do you use cocaine?" Reese asked suddenly.

Frank felt his pulse quickening. He could sense they were going somewhere with this line of questioning. Quickly he said, "Cocaine use is illegal in the state of Oregon."

"I've never used it in Oregon," Rebecca added.

Frank gritted his teeth.

Garrett suddenly burst out laughing. He was mocking her, letting her know that he thought her qualification was obvious. He looked at her as if he could see right through her.

His attitude was starting to get to Frank. He didn't like the angry sound of his own voice as he asked, "Can we move on, please?"

The assistant DA wiped the smirk off his face. "Did Mr. Marsh use cocaine?"

"Never," Rebecca said.

Garrett's eyes narrowed. "The toxicology tests came back positive for cocaine."

There it was. The hook. The reason for all of this. But Rebecca had an answer ready. "Then it's a false positive," she said. "We never did any drugs."

"Not even poppers?" Garrett asked, his eyebrows raised in total disbelief.

"She just told you they didn't use drugs," Frank said forcefully, his irritation building.

They had nothing. They were hounding her, trying to manufacture a case from pixie dust, hoping she'd spill her guts and hand it to them on a platter. At the same time they were openly deprecating, their manner and body language expressing unspoken thoughts. Volumes of them. Their leers said it all.

They were ingrates and they were wrong about Rebecca. Frank was certain of it.

Garrett gave Frank a look of disdain, then turned back to Rebecca and said,

"Because amyl nitrate is often made available to heart patients."

Frank tensed as Garrett watched Rebecca's face for a reaction. Amyl nitrate was an old drug once used in the treatment of angina. That was before nitroglycerine became widely available. Amyl nitrate was hardly the drug of choice for heart patients anymore.

But it *was* used illegally. And it was called a popper, as it was used primarily for sexual enhancement purposes. Purchased on the underground market, the drug was usually inhaled just prior to orgasm. The drug caused the blood vessels to dilate quickly, thereby intensifying the orgasmic sensation. A very dangerous practice.

Garrett continued. "Were you aware of Mr. Marsh's heart condition?"

"He had a little arrhythmia," she answered. "That's not a *heart* condition."

Garrett picked up a yellow legal pad, studied it for a moment, then said, "Mr. Marsh had an advanced case of heart disease."

Rebecca took a deep breath. She seemed taken aback. She glanced at Frank, then gazed at the table vacantly. "He said it wasn't serious."

Her voice was uncertain, almost tentative.

"Why would he have lied to you about it?" Garrett said, pushing.

She shook her head, looking very unsure of herself for the first time.

The room grew silent.

For a moment Rebecca said nothing. She sagged a little in the chair, then caught herself and sat up straight, tugging at the hem of her dress. She looked weary and depressed. Small tears began forming at the corner of her eyes.

She chewed on her lower lip, then choked back a sob. "I never know why men lie," she said. "They just do. Men *lie*."

She said it with such conviction that Garrett was nonplussed. He dropped his gaze and shuffled some papers while he tried to gain back control. Frank smiled at his discomfort. The bastard was too clever by half, but Rebecca was holding up well, her obvious sincerity affecting all of them.

"Would you describe yourself as a dominatrix?" Garrett asked out of the blue.

Frank was infuriated by the question. There was no need for this verbal brutality. Anyone could see Rebecca was suffering.

"Back off this, Bob," he snarled.

Again, Garrett ignored him. "A sadomasochist?" he asked, pushing hard, the leer back on his face.

It was too much. Frank, his face flushed with anger, grabbed Rebecca's elbow, urging her to stand. Confused, she stood up. Frank put a protective arm around her waist.

"The interview's over," he announced. "Do you want to charge her? Go ahead. Otherwise you can contact Miss Carlson through my office."

Garrett shrugged. "Fine."

They were all staring at her, their faces devoid of expression. Then Frank took Rebecca's arm and started toward the door of the interrogation room. Griffin and Reese seemed mesmerized by her sensuous walk. They completely missed Garrett's signal.

"Reese," Garrett barked.

Reese quickly flushed with embarrassment. Frank and Rebecca were almost out the door when they heard him say, "Rebecca Carlson, you're under arrest for the murder of Andrew Marsh."

Frank could hardly believe his ears. He whirled and looked at Garrett, who shrugged sheepishly, like a kid who'd been caught with his hands in the cookie jar.

Then Frank stole a glance at Rebecca. He could see the terror in her eyes. She stood riveted to the floor, her body stiff from shock, her mouth open and her eyes wide.

Quickly the shocked expression changed to a look of pure terror.

Reese was still giving the Miranda warning. "You have the right to remain silent—"

As Reese talked he and Griffin took Rebecca by the arms and escorted her away. She flung her head back and looked over her shoulder at Frank, her expression one of sheer panic.

"Frank!"

She looked small and fragile at that moment, totally confused and vulnerable. Frank's heart sank. He'd let her down terribly. There was no reason, no evidence, nothing that warranted an arrest. It was crazy. Garrett was out of his mind.

"I'll have you out as fast as I can!" he yelled after Rebecca.

He watched until they were out of sight. It was all he could do to not run after them and rip her out of their grasp. Then he turned his attention back to Garrett, who was making a big deal of repacking his briefcase.

Frank was livid. His eyes were like lasers, boring into Garrett's skull. "Trying to get your name on the front page, Bob?" he shouted. "Is that your game?"

Garrett said nothing. He looked at Frank as one would look at a recalcitrant retarded child, a mixture of disdain and sympathy.

"You fucking sandbagged me!" Frank yelled.

Garrett smiled that same cocky smile he'd had last night at the café. "Well," he said, throwing Frank's own words back at him, "don't take it personally."

It was a taunt, and Frank lost his cool right then. Before he could even think, he moved forward, shoving Garrett's chair so hard it skidded back against the wall. There was a *thunk* as Garrett's head smacked the wall.

Garrett stared at Frank in shock. "Jesus, Frank—"

Frank didn't answer. He simply stood there, clenching and unclenching his fists. The assistant DA stood up, rubbed the back of his head, and reached for his briefcase.

"You're spending too much time around criminals," he said calmly. "It affects your judgment."

Then he strode out of the room.

Frank followed him, down the hall and around a corner, then another, the clatter of ancient typewriters and ringing telephones receding in the background.

"You don't have probable cause," Frank said, finally finding his voice.

"Sure I do," Garrett said. "Marsh's will

leaves all ten million dollars to your client, which would have even given *me* a motive."

That was stunning news. Frank fought hard to hide his surprise.

"She admits she was there the night of the murder," Garrett added.

"You don't know if it was homicide," Frank said.

"And the method's self-explanatory," Garrett continued, ignoring Frank's challenge.

"You want to tag her body as the murder weapon?" Frank screamed. "Exhibit A? Is that what she is? It's not a crime to be a great lay."

Garrett grinned. "Good thing, or I'd have to be indicted myself."

The man was becoming insufferable.

"This is a ridiculous case," Frank argued. "Drop the charges. Save the state some money. You can't convict her with what you've got."

Garrett smiled. "In conjunction with cocaine slipped to a rich old man suffering from heart disease? I can make that case."

They'd reached the exit door. Garrett pushed it open and strode down the sidewalk. Frank stayed at his side, still angry, still confused, still trying to get Garrett to reconsider—to no avail.

Garrett was confident, the confidence giving him an edge, making him break out in a wide smile.

"Take your pole out of the water, Frank. The fish ain't biting today. Tell your client she has until the prelim to trade down to a first-degree manslaughter, grab maybe twenty years." He grinned. "She could be out in seven."

Frank's anger threatened to overflow again. "The only time she's ever going to do is what she's doing right this minute. It was a bullshit trick."

Garrett turned to face him, shrugged again, then walked away. "Some balls are tougher to bust than others."

Frank was so angry he rattled off a retort that sounded sophomoric, even to him. But it was the best he could do under the circumstances. "Gee, Bob, thanks for the compliment."

He watched Garrett's back until it was out of sight. Then he looked up. Above him was the famous statue of Portlandia, the second-largest hammered copper statue in the country, the Statue of Liberty being the biggest.

Portlandia, all thirty-six feet of her,

shimmering gold in the morning light with her trident, her grain, her cogwheel, and her sledgehammer, seemed to be reaching down to Frank.

Frank shivered in the cold, damp air, consumed by a sudden sense of ominous foreboding that stayed with him all the way to his car.

**4**

◆Rebecca sat in the holding cell, perched on the edge of a rusty metal bench, looking forlorn and tired, her natural beauty in sharp contrast to the street-weary hardness of the other women in the cell—hookers, drug addicts, thieves, some a combination of all three.

Most of them were regulars who, resenting her beauty, snickered, laughed, and mocked her.

"I hear you offed a guy," one of them said.

Rebecca said nothing.

"What's the matter, cat got your tongue?"

The place smelled of urine, body odor, and stale cigarette smoke. There was spit on the floor and roaches crawling out of a crack in the wall. The place was a hell-hole.

"I hear you're in the movies," another said.

A chorus of laughs. Rebecca ignored them.

One sat beside her and touched her knee. "Don't pay no mind to them."

Rebecca slapped the hand away. "Get the fuck away from me."

Finally, after what seemed like eternity, Rebecca heard footsteps and the sound of jangling keys. A female guard approached the cell and called her name. "Rebecca Carlson!"

Rebecca leaped to her feet, brushed a hand over her wrinkled dress, then fluffed her hair. The others hooted, hollered, and hissed.

"Gettin' out to do some more movies, honey?"

"Hey, how can I get into one of them flicks?"

The guard stuck her key in the cell door, swung it open, and beckoned to Rebecca. "Your lawyer's here."

Rebecca moved quickly out of the cell. She followed the guard down a hallway and into a waiting room. When she saw Frank, she threw herself into his arms and placed her head on his chest.

Frank gripped her arms and gently

pushed her back, looking deep into her tortured eyes. "Are you okay?" he asked.

She shook her head. "It's awful. I can't believe this is happening."

Frank took her arm and escorted her through the labyrinthine hallways and walkways, toward the door of freedom. At the door he stopped. "They're out there," he said quietly. "In force."

"Who?"

"The press. Newspapers, TV, the works. You're big news all of a sudden. We're going to have to find another way out of here."

"Can we?" she said, looking up at him, her eyes pleading.

"Yes, but if they catch up to us, I want you to say nothing. Understand? Not a word."

She took a deep breath, exhaled, then said, "I understand."

She looked so vulnerable he felt a tug from somewhere deep inside him. He was still overwhelmed by her beauty, but it was more than her appearance that attracted him.

While he was aware of her potent sexuality, that sexuality was now subdued, the fires of inner passion banked, repressed by her frightening encounter with the criminal

justice system and all of its inherent
power—a much different kind of power.

Already her face displayed the effects of
a mere few hours spent in jail. It was
drawn, except for the skin under her eyes,
which was puffy and even paler. Her body
language sent a message. She moved with
trepidation instead of confidence.

He wanted to help her.

More than that, he needed to help her.

He took her down some more hallways,
through some doors, and then they were
outside, in the orange glow cast by the setting sun, rushing toward his car. So far they
hadn't been seen.

They made it to the car, where Frank
opened the passenger door and Rebecca
climbed in. The sound of the closing door
alerted one of the photographers idly looking in their direction. He let out a shout.

"There she is!"

"Hey, Dulaney, hold up!"

He and Rebecca were inside his car,
locking the doors. He was shoving the key
in the ignition. The mob was running
toward them, cameramen lugging heavy
equipment, reporters extending their arms,
tape recorders stuck in their hands. A feed-
ing frenzy, with Frank and Rebecca the
blue-plate special.

"What the hell door'd they come out of," he heard one of them shout.

"I hate this shit," another yelled.

"Rebecca!" they all screamed.

"Rebecca!"

They all wanted a piece of her. She was news. Hot news. The juiciest kind of news. News that sent ratings soaring, and set newspapers to pontificating in their editorial pages.

She slumped down in her seat, refusing to look out the window. Frank finally had the engine turning and the car in gear. A reporter reached them and rapped on the window as Frank pulled away.

"Frank!"

Frank ignored him and depressed the accelerator pedal. The car moved forward.

The reporter called after him. "Frank . . . you asshole!"

They were away from them, moving down the street, then another, and finally onto a main thoroughfare.

"You okay?" Frank asked.

She was sitting up now, staring straight ahead, the lights from the oncoming cars playing on her face, giving her eyes an odd appearance.

It was twilight, and ahead, rain clouds were building. Soon it would rain.

"Thank you," she said softly.

"No problem. Was it a little rough in there?"

"Yes."

"It usually is. Let's hope I can prevent that from ever happening again."

She leaned her head back as they continued to drive. For a while neither said anything, both lost in their own thoughts. Then, when he crossed the river and aimed the car south, she said, "I should've moved back to Chicago."

Her voice was wistful.

"Why didn't you?" he asked.

"Because of Andrew."

He had to know. So he asked. "Or because of Andrew's money?"

He saw her reaction out of the corner of his eye. She looked like he'd cut her with a knife. Her mouth was open and her eyes were wide. Her skin seemed even whiter than before. She looked betrayed.

"That's what you'll be hearing in court," he explained, feeling guilty, just as he had the first time they'd met.

"Bob's going to stage a big, ugly trial," he added. "I know the man."

"What's he want?"

"As I told you before, he wants you to plead guilty to first-degree manslaughter."

Some of the hurt left her eyes. "Does he really expect me to plead guilty to spare myself the embarrassment?"

"I don't think so," he said. "I think the offer is for show. I think what he really wants is a trial."

"I'm *not* guilty," she insisted. "I won't plead guilty to anything."

He had to shake her up again, and he did. "I'd feel better if you weren't in the will."

He could hear her intake of breath, the sound of shock.

"Andrew put me in his will?"

Was it an act? He didn't know. He decided to find out. "Don't start jerking me around, Rebecca. You're the sole beneficiary."

She said nothing for a moment, then, "How much?"

Jesus. So much for nobility. He almost laughed out loud. Maybe Sharon was right. Maybe Rebecca would make him a fool after all. Maybe he was being sucked in by a manipulative, scheming . . .

"Wouldn't *you* ask?" she said innocently, as if reading his mind.

He thought for a moment, then said, "Ten million dollars. Give or take."

She turned and looked out the window.

"That looks like a helluva motive."

It was indeed.

"I know how Bob works," he said. "He's going to build his case on your sex life. He'll drag out every dirty little thing you ever did."

"It wasn't dirty," she said, correcting him in a matter-of-fact way.

He shook his head in frustration. "Not to *you*, not to *Andrew*! But people here have straighter views about sex. Anything they don't do themselves is dirty, and believe me, they don't do much."

"That's not true," she said, her confidence quickly returning. They were discussing a subject with which she was most familiar.

"They do it all, Frank. They just don't talk about it. They're all such hypocrites."

He snorted. He hated it when clients thought they understood the human mind. It was bullshit. Juries were unpredictable at best, but in matters of sex, they were always prudish. Always. The ones who understood aggressive sex rarely made it to the jury pool. They found ways to avoid serving on juries.

"Well," he said, "these hypocrites are going to sit in the jury box and listen to Bob say you led Andrew Marsh into perversion."

"I didn't have to lead him anywhere," she said, her voice strong and sure. "Andrew knew what he wanted. He was the most passionate man I ever met. He wanted to explore and I showed him how. What's *wrong* with that?"

"Nothing."

"All we did was make love."

He couldn't resist. "In handcuffs," he added.

She looked at him, then said, "It was different, but it was still making love."

She paused, then asked, "Have you ever seen animals make love, Frank? It's intense, it's violent. But there's such passion."

"We're not animals."

"Yes, we are," she said quietly.

She sounded so sure of herself. He turned and stared at her, seeking a new insight into this strange woman. As it had been the first time he'd seen her, the sexuality was overpowering, fighting off the vulnerability that had cloaked her just minutes ago. The skin that had been white was now flushed with color. She was amazing.

Suddenly she reached for the steering wheel and yanked it. A car horn blared. Very close. Obviously Frank had allowed the car to drift across the center lane.

Rebecca's actions had avoided a head-on collision by inches.

"You're going to kill us, Frank," she said softly.

For the remainder of the trip he paid attention to his driving.

5

◆It had been months since Frank had felt this incredibly turned on.

Every movement of their bodies brought a new sensation. He was obsessed with the moment, the feel of her skin, the firmness of her breasts, the hardness of her nipples, the warmth of her hands, and the smell of her perfume.

A banquet of sexual pleasure.

They were both bathed in sweat, tangled up in the now damp sheets, rolling over each other, clutching each other tightly, their lips and tongues slipping and sliding, their bodies moving with a violent rhythm.

He flicked a nipple with his tongue, then brought his head down slowly, over her flat stomach, stopping to lick her navel, then down to the downy softness between her legs. Expertly he used the tip of his tongue to trace the border of her femininity, then made the circle smaller, slowly drawing closer to the warm, dewy pinkness.

He plunged his tongue within, probing, searching, withdrawing, then reaching in once more.

She gasped with pleasure as she raised her hips to him.

He reached up with both hands, gently massaging her nipples as his tongue tantalized her, made her gasp for air, brought her senses fully alive.

She groaned with bliss as she tousled his hair, then pulled him away.

"My turn," she said breathlessly.

He smiled and lay on his back.

She started by kissing him on the lips, then flicking her tongue and sliding wet lips over his chest, playfully placing her teeth on his nipples, then down to his stomach.

She took his erection in her hand, stroked it gently, then placed her lips over the tip. At the same time she moved her body so that she was straddling him, exposing herself inches from his mouth.

He responded in kind.

She rolled away and turned her body, her eyes glazed with lust, her arms beckoning.

He entered her again, stoking slowly,

hearing her soft moans in his ears, feeling her hot breath on his shoulder, the smell of her strong in his nostrils.

He felt her heel pressing against his back, urging him on, and he thrust himself deeper inside her. He was close now, too close. He pulled back and took her breast in his mouth, his tongue flicking at the nipple. He heard her moan with pleasure.

His skin felt electrically charged. Hers felt like fine silk. The palms of his hands massaged the lovely swell of her buttocks while he brought his head down, his tongue rolling inside her navel. Then away and down, to the softness between her legs.

Again, she moaned.

She, too, was close.

He entered her gently, stroking slowly, his hands squeezing her buttocks, then releasing, then squeezing again. She cried out in pleasure, pushing herself forward, holding him close as she reached orgasm.

Her body shuddered as she groaned with satisfaction, first one, then once again, the two almost violent orgasms coming back-to-back. A rarity for her.

He waited for a moment, then moved his mouth back to her breasts. He felt her drive her heel into his back, urging him back inside. He responded, and as soon as he felt the familiar, welcoming warmth, he knew he was done.

He exploded with almost forgotten fury, his body arched, his teeth clenched, his whole being concentrated in that sweet, delicious, magical geography nestled perfectly between her long legs.

Spent, he eased back, rolling his hips in small, fond circles, not wanting it to end. She kneaded his back as she fought to bring her breathing under control, then let her legs slide off his back.

For a moment he rested his head on her breasts, listening to the pounding of her heart, feeling his own heart banging hard against his rib cage.

Sharon laughed, her voice shallow under his weight. "You're great when a big trial gets close."

He rolled off her.

"How about the rest of the time?" he asked.

"You know what I mean," she said.

Suddenly the tender mood was broken. She was putting him down again. "No, I don't know what you mean," he said accusingly.

Sharon didn't answer. She rolled out of bed, her buttocks rippling as she walked to the bathroom. "I'm going to take a shower," she said.

She left him there, thinking, listening to the sounds of the shower, still smelling her in his nostrils, feeling her hands on him, and her tongue, and her mouth—

When they'd first married, they'd had a habit of falling asleep in each other's arms. Now it was different. Now sex almost had to be scheduled. And when it was over, there was no sense of mellowness, no relaxed savoring of the intimacy, just a short break, then back to the routine of living.

He tried to rationalize it. There was the crazy work schedule, for one thing. When they were together, one or the other was exhausted much of the time. Then there was the normal waning of passion that takes place between long-married people. He figured that was a factor, too.

Still, he wondered if there wasn't something more significant involved. Other couples they knew had frantic work schedules and they managed to find the time for sex. With Sharon, other things were more important.

Well, he thought, at least tonight had been a winner. With the Rebecca Carlson trial just days away, he was inspired. Tonight, he'd waited for Sharon to come home from work, rare for him, and he'd been ready with some champagne and a single red rose, sitting there in the kitchen naked, a smile on his face. He was hard to resist.

Odd, how a big trial became an aphrodisiac to him. He'd often wondered about it, trying to figure it out. Was it the power—or the trust placed in him by the clients?

If he was good, as good as he could be, the client had a chance, unless the evidence was so strong that going to trial was virtually redundant. But when the facts were ambiguous, murky, conflicting, or even open to misinterpretation, a trial was definitely indicated.

Then it was Frank's intellect and experience allied against the forces of the criminal justice system. In effect, one man against a mob—the establishment Mafia.

The mob, as he called them, had unlimited resources. They could spend whatever it took to win a big case. They could bring in experts, put a dozen investigators on the streets, turn over every rock.

Frank's resources were limited to those of the client, unless he wanted to invest his own money. Occasionally he did, but it was bad business.

But if the client was rich, Frank could use that money to prepare a defense properly.

If the client was poor, however, the state never paid enough for a lawyer to conduct a thorough investigation. It was one reason the prisons were full of poor people.

Already, this case—the Carlson case—had cost over sixty thousand dollars, the money used to take depositions, file a dozen motions, spend hours in court on pretrial hearings, even hire two shrinks to provide expert testimony if needed. And the actual trial was yet to begin.

For the last five months Frank had pulled out all the stops. Nothing had worked. Garrett was intractable, irrevocably committed to a big, splashy trial. For some reason, even with a shaky case, Garrett ground inexorably toward a show trial. The man was letting his ego get in the way, looking for a big score, anticipating the expected sleazy testimony to turn the jury against Rebecca.

Maybe it would.

Frank had to prevent that from happening.

That was the thrill. Beating the odds. That, and knowing that a human being had given him the responsibility for defending him or her from the superior forces of the mob.

Often, as in this case, someone's very life depended on Frank, and they had to trust him with it, just like a very sick patient undergoing an operation had to trust the surgeon.

He'd heard that surgeons were the horniest men of all. Some operated almost every day, the stimulus of life-and-death decisions stoking their libido constantly.

He groaned. It would kill him. Frank was in court much less frequently, but trials made him hot. No question. It was more than enough.

When he awoke, he was alone in bed, a bed now bathed in light from the rising sun. He was astonished. He'd slept the night away.

He heard Sharon in the bathroom. He pulled himself out of bed and joined her.

She was sitting at the makeup table, wearing a black-and-green push-up bra that exposed much of her creamy-white breasts. Instead of regular panties, she wore a simple thong. He felt the tumescence returning. God, he really *was* horny.

"Is that for me?" he asked, grinning like a fool.

She looked at his reflection in the mirror and smiled. He leaned over, kissed her shoulder, and plucked at her thong. He was already fully erect. He couldn't remember the last time he'd recharged his batteries so quickly.

Sharon noted his exposed ardor and said, "Sweetie, I'm late. It's after eight already."

Then she stood up and walked past him, like he wasn't there.

He followed her into the bedroom, his erection fading fast. "You don't need to be there every single goddamn minute," he exclaimed.

She ignored the comment and began to dress.

"Well?"

"Yeah, I do," she said. "I'm the boss, I'm the owner, I'm in charge."

"So what! Give it a rest, dammit. You worked last night until late. I waited for you. Now, at the break of dawn, you have to go back? What's so damn important at this hour?"

She looked at him coldly. "I don't have to explain my actions to you. I don't like it when you get up at seven in the morning and leave me in bed. But you're a lawyer, you work days. And I've worked nights ever since you met me. After twelve years of nights, you could be used to it."

"I'm not," he said softly.

She spoke in measured tones, quietly, but with conviction. "My father put you through law school with that café, when it was nothing but a sandwich shop. That's a *lot* of sandwiches, Frank."

There it was again, the haughtiness rising up in her, the superior attitude he hated so much, the veiled claim that he'd be nothing if it hadn't been for her father.

Yes, her father had helped him get through law school, and he was grateful. And when he'd become a prosecutor, he'd paid her father back with interest. She never mentioned that. She never mentioned how hard he worked to make it through law school, how much he'd given up. Just the money. Always the money.

Her father had died and left her a going concern, and to be sure, she'd turned it into something special, but she never expressed the thought that *her* success was due in part to her father's efforts. That she took for granted. But his success was somehow tainted and he was never allowed to forget it.

"He should have put me through cooking school," Frank said sarcastically. "Maybe then I'd have seen you more."

She was completely dressed now, her

clothes hip but not sexy. Almost a uniform, the old threads of another era.

The expression on her face signaled a message. She was tolerating his outburst, speaking to him as she would to an unreasonable child. Condescending. And he hated it.

"I love my work," she said. "So do you. That's why we *do* it."

He was furious. Rather than continue the argument, he turned away from her and switched on the television set. "Don't let me keep you," he said coldly.

She turned on her heel and walked back to the bathroom.

◆As he drove to the office Frank pushed the simmering anger and resentment from his thoughts and forced himself to concentrate on the Carlson case. The trial was almost upon him and there was no time to lose. He ran several ideas over in his mind, wanting to sort things out.

Today was to be an important day. There was the scheduled deposition with Marsh's secretary, Joanne Braslow, long delayed for one excuse or another. He fully expected Garrett would be there as well. The assistant DA could have sent someone else, but Frank doubted he'd do it. The bastard seemed to be enjoying the prosecution of Rebecca, as though it were something personal. Unusual for Garrett.

When Frank arrived at the office, he called Biggs into his office. The investigator took a seat across from Frank and listened intently. He had an offhand way about him, but his mind ticked like a fine old watch.

"I told you once before that you don't get as rich as Marsh was by being a nice guy," Frank said. "I asked you to find out who he fucked over . . . business, social, personal. Who else wanted him turned into worm food? You've given me nothing."

Biggs nodded. "I've been doing my best. Fact is, there isn't much. I'm now hitting all the dealers with a list of the nearest and dearest. . . . See if we can turn up a user."

"Good," Frank said.

They ran over some other ideas, and then Gabe Weider, Frank's junior partner, was standing at the office doorway.

"Yes?"

"Joanne Braslow's here," Gabe said. "Garrett brought doughnuts. They're in the conference room."

"The man's considerate," Frank said dryly.

He and Biggs stood up. As Biggs walked away the black man said of Garrett, "He always eats them all."

Frank smiled. Biggs was very observant. A good quality in an investigator.

◆  ◆  ◆

The conference room was spacious and well furnished, overlooking the Willamette River, which cut the city in half. Positioned beside Frank's corner office, the room allowed a view of much of the city of Portland.

He'd paid extra so as to enjoy this view, especially the one from his own private office, and considered the money well spent.

Like the rest of the law office, the conference room was well appointed, an appropriate reflection of Frank's success.

At the moment the oval mahogany table was littered with china cups, napkins, and spoons. A box of doughnuts sat in the middle of the table.

Once some of the mess was cleared away, they got down to business.

Everyone was in place. A court reporter hired for the occasion sat at one end of the table, her fingers poised over her shorthand machine. On one side of the table, Garrett and Joanne. Across from them, Frank and Gabe.

They were ready.

Joanne looked somewhat demure, but still attractive. She was dressed conservatively in a plain drab brown dress that did nothing for her. Her reddish-brown hair framed a pleasant face, one that reflected intelligence. Her dark eyes were her most arresting feature, but she wore little make-up, as if trying hard to downplay their impact. She looked uptight and repressed, possibly sexually repressed.

Give her a morning at Elizabeth Arden and she'd come out looking like a million dollars, Frank thought. It wouldn't do much for what lay inside, though. For that, she'd need a shrink.

Frank began with the unimportant stuff, the basic information relating to the witness. "For the record, would you state your name and address?"

She did as she was asked.

"How long have you worked for Mr. Marsh?"

"Six years."

"And what were your duties?"

"I was his personal secretary," she said proudly.

"Did you discover Mr. Marsh's body?"

A flash of pain in her eyes. "Yes, I did."

"Where did you discover the body?"

"He was in his bed. Lying on his back."

"Was he handcuffed?"

She seemed repelled by the question. "No."

"Otherwise restrained?"

"No."

"How did you know he was dead?"

She took a deep breath, looked away for a moment, then said, "I didn't. I thought he had fallen asleep. When I tried to wake him, I realized he was dead and called the police."

Frank looked at the notes he'd jotted down on a yellow legal pad earlier. "Did you make it a habit to enter his bedroom?" he asked.

"No. When he wasn't in his office, I called him on the intercom. When I received no answer, I thought something was wrong."

"Why?"

"Well, his car was still at the house, and he would normally leave a note for me if he wasn't going to be there."

"So you went up to the bedroom."

"Not at first. I looked around the other rooms first."

"Why?"

Now she looked truly in pain. "I knew Mr. Marsh had a bad heart," she said softly. "I thought perhaps he'd fainted."

She seemed sincere enough.

They took five minutes covering more of the nonessential stuff, just for the record. Now it was time to get to the meat and potatoes. Frank looked at his notes, then at Joanne.

"How well do you know Rebecca Carlson?" he asked.

At mention of the name, Joanne's body stiffened and her eyes became slits. "I would say hello to Rebecca when I came to the house, but that was about it. We didn't . . . chat."

"Did you disapprove of their relationship?" Frank asked.

Joanne looked as if she'd just stepped in something left behind by a stray dog. "It wasn't normal," she said, almost spitting the words out. "They didn't have normal sex."

Frank found that comment interesting. There was the infamous videotape, of course, but the woman sounded as if she knew much more.

"How do you know what kind of sex they had?" he asked.

She stiffened even more in the chair, her hands gripping the arms so tightly her knuckles turned white. For some reason Frank wondered if she'd ever had sex at all, then pushed the thought from his mind.

"I wasn't looking through the keyhole, if that's what you're implying," she said emphatically. "I'd come to the house to pick up papers or speak to Andrew. I'd find their little toys all over the place."

The word *toys* was uttered with unequivocal loathing.

Frank almost smiled. She didn't appear to be able to control her feelings. If she was going to be a witness for Garrett, he felt sure he could show her bias.

"Would it be accurate to characterize your feelings toward my client as negative?"

"I don't have much sympathy for drug users," she snapped.

Now she was beginning to piss him off. Her high-mindedness was worn like a badge of honor, as if she was better than everyone else.

"Do you have any *personal* knowledge that she used drugs?" he asked.

She was eager to answer the question, as if she had been waiting for it to be asked. "I *personally* saw her shovel the stuff up her nose. Is that good enough?"

Frank was flabbergasted, but he didn't let it show. He was aware that Garrett was observing him closely, looking for a reaction. Only Frank's eye twitched, almost imperceptibly.

He heard Gabe shifting around nervously in his chair and made a mental note to talk to him about it later. The kid had much to learn about this game.

Now he understood why this deposition had been so long in coming. Garrett was pulling the strings behind the scenes, giving Frank little time before the opening of the trial to counter this potentially devastating testimony.

"In front of a secretary?" Frank asked pointedly. "Your statement is that Rebecca snorted cocaine in front of you?"

Joanne sat firm. "I was at the house one morning. I thought she was still upstairs with him. I went into the powder room, and she was spooning up coke from one of those little vials."

Frank pressed her. "What did she say when she saw you?"

"She didn't know I was there."

"Really," he said. "How convenient. How *big* is this powder room?" he asked, his voice filled with incredulity.

Joanne didn't answer the question. Instead she said, "She was too busy to notice."

"Did you tell your boss what you'd seen?"

"No."

"Why not?"

She answered in anger. "I wanted to

keep my job. And that didn't include telling him his girlfriend was a cokehead slut."

The room fell silent, save for the sound of Joanne's heavy breathing. She glared at Frank and he glared right back.

"Frank?"

Frank turned and looked at Garrett, who was wearing that cocky smile of his again.

"Why don't you take the last doughnut?"

Frank needed to talk to Rebecca. Now. Too many questions still remained unanswered, and too many of Rebecca's statements now seemed false.

Joanne's deposition had been a tough one. She was going to make a terrific witness for the prosecution and Garrett knew it.

The assistant DA had goaded Frank throughout the depo, sure of his position now that the trial was near. Even Sharon's words of warning kept ringing in his ears. Frank would be made to look a fool, she'd said when he'd first taken this case. He wondered if she might be right.

He drove directly from his office to the gallery that Rebecca owned, not bothering to call ahead, hoping to find her unprepared for the many questions he was going to ask.

He found the place, parked the car, and bolted through the front door of the place.

The large floor area, formerly a clothing store, was divided into small rooms for more intimate viewing of the hundreds of photographs on display. In one of the rooms, some workmen were busy moving a false wall for a new exhibition. Frank couldn't see the workmen, but he could hear them, cursing and drilling and hammering. A cloud of dust hung in front of halogen lights fixed on some featured photographs.

He went from room to room looking for Rebecca, calling out her name, barely able to be heard above the din. He finally saw her in the mezzanine. She was looking down at him, watching silently. His rage erupted.

"You fucking lied to me!" he screamed at her. "You lied on *tape*. You were asked a direct question. 'Do *you* use cocaine.' That was bullshit."

"I didn't lie," she said.

"The hell you didn't. They have an eyewitness who's going to testify that not only do you *use* it, you used it in Marsh's house."

She stared at him for a moment, then

slowly walked down the stairs, like someone making an entrance at a black-tie banquet. Halfway down, during a momentary pause in the racket, she said, "Joanne's lying."

The hammers started pounding again. "I didn't say it was Joanne," he bellowed, trying to be heard above the din.

She was now on the main floor, standing in front of him, looking up into his face, the epitome of wounded honor and pure innocence. "Who else would've been in his house while I was there?" she asked.

"Do you know the expression 'smoking gun'?" he asked, almost spitting out the words.

"She was in love with him!" she exclaimed, finally showing some emotion. "She wants to see me punished. Not for killing him, but for loving him. Don't you see?"

He glared at her. "Andrew must have been a pretty goddamn lovable guy. Everybody was in *love* with him!"

She was looking hurt again. "I haven't touched coke since I was seventeen."

He wasn't convinced. "She makes a good witness," he said. "She may hate your guts, but she looks so pure the jury may well buy what she's saying."

Rebecca said nothing for a moment.

"You're supposed to be my lawyer. Why is it you always think I'm lying to you? I have no reason to lie to my lawyer. Only idiots lie to their lawyers. I know that much."

"Like I said," he repeated, "she makes a very credible witness."

"And you believe *her*."

"I didn't say that."

"You imply it."

"Look, I'm trying to explain something to you. When it comes down to it, it's her word against yours on the coke issue. Who will the jury believe? I'd be less than honest if I told you they'll throw out her testimony at face value. I need something more than 'I don't do coke.' That just isn't enough."

She stood there glaring at him, breathing hard, her breasts heaving underneath her tight sweater. Once again, he felt himself affected by her magnificence. He worked hard to focus on her eyes, feeling the dust tickling his nostrils.

"I want you to come meet somebody," she said suddenly, moving past him.

"Who?"

"You have your car?"

Frank shook his head. "Forget it. I don't have time for games."

She turned and fixed him with a withering stare. "This is no game, Frank. This is my *life*. Are you my lawyer or aren't you?"

She grabbed her trench coat and strode out of the gallery. Without waiting for him, she jerked open the passenger's door and slid in, slamming the door behind her.

Frank, still seething, got in the car beside her.

She directed him to Portland's Chinatown, through the intricately carved gate at N.W. Fourth and Burnside that marked the entrance to this part of the city.

"Park anywhere here," she said curtly.

He pulled over, parked the car, and got out, leaving her to open her own door. He didn't feel like being a gentleman. She glared at him through the windshield for a moment, then got out and walked briskly down the sidewalk.

Like Chinatowns everywhere, the stores all seemed jammed together. The air was thick with the smell of cooking oils and food. Steam from a laundry surrounded a forest of garbage bins and stray cats looking for something to eat.

It had started to rain. Perfect, thought Frank. It matched his dark mood.

Rebecca walked ahead of him and turned into a doorway. Frank followed her into a dimly lit store and closed the slightly warped wooden door behind him. He heard the tinkle of a bell in the distance.

It was warm inside the store, its walls lined with ancient-looking glass-fronted cabinets filled with jars and vials in every size and shape, all labeled with names of various herbs or animal parts. In the middle of the floor, more cabinets were arranged in a haphazard fashion.

Odd smells assailed Frank's nostrils, a strange mixture of the sweet and the pungent. Above him, three unlit naked low-watt bulbs hung suspended from the ceiling.

Still fighting his rage, Frank wandered around the store, peeking at the countless items, aware that Rebecca was watching him intently. The hell with it. This was her party. Let her explain what the hell they were doing there.

A small Chinese man emerged from the back of the store, his face lighting up as he recognized Rebecca.

"Hello, Becky."

"Hello, Raymond. I want you to meet Frank Dulaney. He's my lawyer."

Frank gave the Chinese proprietor a desultory nod.

"This is Dr. Wong," Rebecca said, her voice void of any emotion.

"A pleasure to meet you, Mr. Dulaney. You are most welcome here."

Frank nodded again. Rebecca turned to the man. "Would you show him what you give me?" she requested.

Dr. Wong appeared perplexed. He gave Frank a look, then nodded. "Of course," he said softly.

He walked slowly to one of the cabinets, unlocked it, and removed a small vial of white powder, spoon attached. He uncapped the vial and offered it to Frank.

Frank, stunned, reeled back. "You gotta be kidding."

Rebecca was staring at him, a whisper of derision in her eyes. "Go ahead," she said evenly. "You said I was a liar. Well, investigate."

Reluctantly Frank dipped his finger in the white powder, then brought his finger to his mouth. The taste was unusual, but it wasn't cocaine. He knew that much.

Confused now, he looked at Rebecca and asked, "What the hell is this?"

Rebecca's face broke into a grin. She put her hand to her mouth and started giggling like a schoolgirl, delighted with Frank's obvious discomfort.

The Chinese man answered the question, speaking to Frank as he might speak to a child. "It's Chinese peony root," he said.

Frank was stunned. "Peony root? What the hell is peony root?"

"It's an aspirin substitute," the man answered.

Rebecca, still smiling, said, "Tell him what it's for."

Dr. Wong nodded and said, "She suffers from dysmenorrhea."

The word meant nothing to Frank.

"Cramps," Rebecca explained.

"Cramps?"

"Cramps."

It was ludicrous. He *was* a fool. At the same time he felt enormous relief. There was a logical answer after all. A witness, in fact. Someone who could testify as to why Rebecca was sniffing a white powder. The jury might not buy it, but then again—

For a moment he got angry again. She could have simply told him. Instead she'd chosen to show him in a most dramatic fashion.

But then he understood why.

She could read him pretty well. He'd called her a liar, a pretty strong indication he didn't trust her. She wanted him to remember more than just an explanation. She wanted him to experience his mistake.

He started to laugh. As sweet relief flooded his body, the laugh became near hysterical, making his body shake. He kept turning in small circles, barely able to breathe.

So stupid. So incredibly stupid. She'd been using peony root for her problem with cramps. Not cocaine. He was her lawyer, yet he was constantly accusing her of lying to him. Each time she had an explanation. The confluence of relief and remorse made him giddy.

The phone in the back of the store rang. Dr. Wong left to answer it, leaving Frank with Rebecca and his expanding sensation of chagrin.

Rebecca could see it on his face, but she wanted to stick the knife in a little deeper.

"You're supposed to be on my side," she said. "You could have at least given me the benefit of the doubt."

"You're right," he said.

At the sound of the rain hitting the glass windows in heavy sheets, Frank turned toward the front door. The car was at least forty feet away. They'd both be soaked.

Again, as if reading his mind, Rebecca said, "Do you mind waiting fifteen minutes?"

"Not at all."

She gave him a small smile, then walked away, toward one of several cubicles at the back of the store. Frank wandered around while he waited, looking at various items, shaking his head in wonderment that people would actually take some of this stuff. Just the thought of it turned his stomach.

The store was quite dark. No lights had been switched on during the rainstorm. Frank almost stumbled over a large vase on the floor but quickly regained his balance. As if searching for safety, he moved toward the soft fluorescent light in one of the cubicles. Silently he crept forward, then peered over the carved wooden screen to where Rebecca lay facedown on a padded table, partially naked, her muscular torso defined by an exotic mixture of shadow and light.

Frank caught his breath as he watched Dr. Wong begin his work, embedding long, silvery needles into Rebecca's back then twirling each one several times before he continued. Rebecca remained motionless, her chest rising and falling in a steady rhythm. Her face was turned the other way, so Frank stared openly, entranced.

The skin on her back was like the skin on her face, perfect, flawless. Her back was beautiful, strong and muscular, with a curve to it that brought back memories of the videotape he'd seen at least ten times.

As he watched, his mind's eye replayed the tape. He saw Rebecca astride Andrew Marsh, her body covered in sweat, her head tossed back as she drove the man inside her.

Yes, she liked to dominate a man. That much was clear. But Marsh had been old and in failing health. Would she act that way with a man who was young, strong, and healthy? Was it simply her need to dominate or was she looking for a man who was capable of taming her?

Looking at her now, submitting her body to the thin silver needles of Dr. Wong, she seemed quite passive. The muscles in her back were relaxed, the skin smooth and supple.

He felt himself growing hard.

"Is it still raining?" she asked softly.

Frank was shaken from his reverie. She seemed to know he was staring at her.

"Yes," he said.

She slowly turned her head and looked at him. "Can you drive me home?"

"I'll be happy to," he said immediately.

He wandered about the store as he waited for her to get dressed. Outside, the rain continued to pound the pavement, the passing cars throwing up small rooster tails of spray as they drove by.

He thought about Sharon.

Last night, he'd tried to be romantic, behaving like a newlywed with the flower and his nakedness. She'd responded, yes, but as soon as the sex was over, she'd switched Frank off and turned her thoughts to more important matters.

Always, there were more important matters.

She was being superior, discounting Frank's contribution to their marriage—using him, in fact. Everything was geared to make it easier for Sharon. Frank was doing all the compromising, all the giving, while Sharon was taking.

It wasn't right.

And then this morning, she'd thrown her father at him again. Another put-down. Another expression of where he stood in the big picture.

Rebecca was in business, too. Yet she seemed to have time for other things.

Jesus.

He had to stop thinking about Rebecca in those terms.

"I'm ready," Rebecca said behind him.

He turned and looked into her long-lashed eyes. Her skin seemed to glow in the dimness, her eyes shining, her vitality restored by Dr. Wong's treatment. The doctor stood quietly behind her, a thin knowing smile on his lips.

Frank nodded to the doctor, opened the door, and he and Rebecca dashed through the rain.

They drove in silence, each lost in their own thoughts. But Frank was aware of her nearness. He could smell the ointment that Dr. Wong had applied to her back, a spicy concoction of some kind that served to block the aroma of her normal perfume.

It wasn't unpleasant, just different.

The windshield wipers squealed noisily as they drove in silence. He thought about turning on the car radio, but for some reason was afraid to. He felt strange, somehow removed from the present.

She lived in a houseboat on the river, and by the time they got there, it was twilight. Frank played the part of a gentleman as he held the umbrella over Rebecca's head while they walked to the front door of her houseboat.

It was as big as an average house, two stories high, with a sliding glass door off the upper bedroom that led to a large deck. Below that, another deck, fitted with chairs and a table, and a large umbrella.

"I've never been in one of these things,"

he said, examining the exterior of her houseboat.

She looked at him, her eyes wide, her lips slightly parted. "Here's your chance."

The way she said it gave him pause. He sensed she was offering more than just a guided tour of the houseboat. He felt a tinge of guilt, and when she opened the door and went inside, he stayed behind on the dock.

She looked at him, the question in her eyes.

"It's a bad idea," he said simply.

"Why?"

"I'm your lawyer. It just doesn't look right."

She lowered her gaze and said, "What if you weren't my lawyer?"

There were a hundred thoughts running through his mind. She was provocative and appealing, at once dangerous and inviting. There was a touch of pure evil about her, but there was also the promise of adventure, of something almost supernatural, of experiences most men can only dream about. He could see it in her eyes and hear it in her voice.

Again, as he had in the Chinese doctor's store, he replayed the videotape in his mind. He saw Rebecca sitting atop Andrew

Marsh, devoid of inhibitions, enthralled with the act of sex itself. He saw her exult in it, almost worship it, her body constantly moving, giving and getting pleasure, excluding the world for the moment.

He loved Sharon, but he was also a man. Like every man, he fantasized from time to time. And right now he was fantasizing about making it with Rebecca, aware that his fantasy could be made reality if he so chose.

He felt the hardness returning.

He wanted her. But there was danger in that, he knew. Not just because she was a client, but because it was wrong for a dozen reasons, the most profound of which was her unique power, unlike anything in his experience. Her power—a visceral, emasculating domination—truly frightened him. Yet he saw the ultimate promise in her eyes, and his fear was tinged with a strange excitement.

"It would look even worse," he said.

Rebecca held his gaze, taking the measure of him. Then she glanced down the street, first one way, then the other. She fixed her gaze on Frank once more. "Nobody's looking."

He had to move. Now. If he didn't move now, he was lost. He knew that, but his legs seemed not to be a part of him. It took a supreme effort to get them to obey his orders.

Finally he was moving away.

"Good night, Rebecca," he said, his voice sounding hollow.

He heard her behind him. "Frank . . . how often do you make love to your wife?"

He turned and saw her standing in the doorway, smiling.

Jesus.

Was he wearing a sign? Or was it that she knew instinctively because of who she was and what she was. A woman to whom no man was much of a mystery—another element of her strange power.

"All the time," he said.

"Liar."

He wasn't offended. It was her turn, and she never seemed to miss an opportunity to turn the tables.

"See you in court tomorrow," he said.

That brought her back to reality. He could see her body stiffen.

"Okay," she said weakly.

"Are you scared?" he asked.

"Not if you tell me I shouldn't be."

He smiled at her. "We're gonna kick their ass!"

He turned away and walked down the

dock, his footsteps sounding hard against the wooden planks of the dock. As he strode to his car Frank felt pretty good about himself. He'd been sorely tempted, but had restrained himself. That made him proud.

And when he got to his car and looked back at the houseboat, watching it sitting serenely in the water, the last vestiges of the day's light giving it a warm orange glow, he still felt proud.

But he was hard again.

◆It was a great day for the start of a trial. The air was cool, but the sun was bright. The gray marble steps leading from the street to the courthouse gleamed, the long shadows cast by the majestic pillars in front looking like giant black fingers.

From the start, the press was there in force, the locals sharing space with the out-of-towers from the big cities. Trucks filled with electronic equipment and sporting large parabolic dishes on their roofs were parked in the street, protected by local police officers.

Thick black cables snaked from truck to truck, spilling over onto the sidewalks. Stocky men and women carrying heavy minicams roamed the area like locusts, sound technicians trailing behind, connected to their camera people like mountain climbers, earphones pressed to their heads.

The trial had become a cause célèbre because of its story, a tale almost as old as humanity itself—a supposedly heartless, beautiful woman accused of seducing, then murdering an older man for his money. The public couldn't get enough.

There were so many press people, court officials held a lottery for daily passes giving entry into the small courtroom. Those without passes milled about on the street, hoping their luck would change tomorrow.

For Frank and Rebecca, going to and from court involved running a gauntlet. The enemy was everywhere, covering every entry to the building. Cameras, microphones, and tape recorders were thrust in Rebecca's and Frank's face while people screamed questions, most of which were downright obnoxious.

Other than a short statement that his client was innocent, which he made that first day, Frank refrained from any other dialogue with the press. With the screaming tabloid headlines already finding his client guilty, reasonable discourse was impossible, and anything he said would be distorted. It was best to say nothing at all.

After the experience of that first morning, Frank started parking in the under-

ground garage and taking the elevator up
to the floor where the courtrooms were
located. There was still a gauntlet, but it
was much smaller, confined to the corridor, and the distance from the elevator
bank to the courtroom was almost bear-
able.

Voir dire, the picking of a jury, took a
day and a half. Both lawyers qualified
prospective jurors carefully, using the latest
psychological profiling techniques. Frank
asked questions designed to root out those
who appeared not to have formed an opinion about the case, but harbored attitudes
that would be prejudicial to Rebecca.

At the same time he was restricted by
the laws governing the picking of juries. He
had to accept the verbal answer and rely
on body language, eye contact, even occu-
pational choices to determine if the
prospective juror was wrong for Rebecca.

Librarians, for example. Or, authority
figures such as managers or schoolteachers.
These kinds of people had a tendency to be
rigid thinkers, organized and somewhat
insensitive to those outside life's main-
stream, especially when it came to sexual
mores.

But with limited preemptory challenges available to both lawyers, dismissing a juror for cause was best, and unless the candidates were forthcoming, cause was out of the question. The questions, therefore, became arduous.

In the end, neither lawyer got exactly the jury he would have liked, but both felt they had successfully precluded some people with a strong bias in favor of his opponent. Only time would tell.

Rebecca was proving to be her own worst enemy. Despite Frank's many impassioned entreaties, even appeals to her logic, Rebecca had flatly refused to tone down her appearance. In every way, she looked extremely sexy, exactly the opposite of the image Frank wanted her to project.

Her hair was whipped to perfection around her head, accentuating her sultry eyes and full lips. She was dressed in an elegant soft brown dress that clung to her body like a second skin.

She was innocent, she kept saying, and that was all that mattered. If he was any good as a lawyer, he'd convince them of that truth.

He talked to her about perceptions, about prejudice and bias, about the fact that her stubbornness could result in a guilty verdict based on her appearance alone. It wasn't that juries were stupid, he explained. It was that they were composed of *people*, and people made mistakes.

If her appearance made them think of her as less than upstanding, everything said would be filtered through that first impression. If she was perceived as an anti-establishment sexual freak, most of the testimony on her behalf would fall on deaf ears.

Nothing reached her. She was who she was, she said. She refused to be—in her terms—a hypocrite. They would have to accept her as she was. That was it.

Angry, he told her those on the jury could do as they liked, and she would be the one who paid for it. Not him. Even that failed to move her, and he found her intractability puzzling and frustrating.

Rebecca was a survivor, but on this issue she was allowing herself to be victimized by her own beauty. Why? he wondered. She was no fool. He'd learned that much these past few months. Why was she so resolute? Was it simply ego?

Now, with voir dire finally complete, they were ready to go. Frank felt the usual tingle in the pit of his stomach and the slight rush of adrenaline in his veins. It was always like this at the start of a major trial.

To some, it would be a concern. Not so with Frank. It was a familiar and welcome sensation. He would have been concerned had he not felt nervous. Stage fright sharpened his senses, made him more alert and focused.

Garrett was seated at the prosecutor's table, the very same table in the very same courtroom they'd used the last time. That time Frank had beaten him badly. He could see Garrett was itching to even the score.

He was dressed in a new suit, a conservative blue pinstripe cut in American fashion, but one that again failed to hide his muscular body. His highly starched white shirt accentuated the red tie. The power tie. The one with the little Stars and Stripes embroidered all over it.

As always, Garrett received admiring glances from most of the women in the room, including those seated in the jury box.

For this trial, Frank wore a suit of almost the same cut and style as Garrett's. Like Garrett, he wore a white shirt, eschewing the normal blue shirts he preferred. And, like Garrett, he wore the power tie, a red one, but without the embroidered flags.

What the hell. There was a limit.

Frank noticed a young, plain-faced woman sitting in the second chair beside Garrett. Frank didn't know who she was, but she certainly didn't appear impressive. Maybe she was a psychologist, the one who'd helped Garrett pick the jury. It didn't matter. Garrett was his main adversary. Frank would deal with the woman if need be.

Rebecca sat with Frank at the defense table. Gabe sat in a chair behind them, his status reduced to nothing more than errand boy on this one. He took it well. He was still the student, still learning, still absorbing.

The room buzzed in anticipation. The first few rows were filled with reporters, the rest with spectators. All of the wood in the room had been freshly shined, and the smell of furniture polish hung in the air like a cloud. Even the brass railings on the bench and the jury box gleamed. Someone had realized the city of Portland was now in the public eye. They wanted to present a good image.

Judge Mabel Burnham presided, which was a break. She was in her fifties, tough, somewhat flamboyant, but confident, and most important, fair. The black woman was an experienced jurist with a reputation for taking no crap from anyone. Frank figured that was a strike against Garrett right there.

"All rise!"

It was about to begin. Frank felt a sudden jolt of adrenaline.

Judge Burnham took her seat, as did everyone else, then got right down to business.

"I can't change the titillating nature of this trial," she said, "but if I'd wanted to work in a circus, I'd have learned how to ride a trapeze. I am not going to put up with any performances by counsel or by the gallery. I'm imposing a gag order—"

There was a rumble in the gallery. The judge was smiling at the reporters.

"Which I always enjoy."

They quieted down. The judge looked at Frank, then Garrett. "The only quotes I expect to see are from admitted testimony, or I'll blame you personally. I'll come down with both feet, is that clear as day?"

First Garrett, then Frank nodded assent.

"Are the people ready to proceed, Mr. Garrett?"

Garrett stood up. "Yes, Your Honor."

"Very well."

Garrett took a deep breath, exhaled,

then took his position in front of the jury box. He looked splendid, confident, and a little offended.

Frank knew the ploy well.

During voir dire, while the lawyers asked questions of the potential jurors, the attention was on them, not the defendant. They were engaged in their own minitrial, and most wanted to win their case and remain on the jury. To be excused was a form of rejection that many took quite personally.

But with the opening statements, the jurors were concentrating not on themselves but on the lawyers, the judge, the defendant, the witnesses, and the physical evidence. They were imbued with a fresh sense of grave responsibility, and they usually took it seriously.

Garrett, by using facial expressions, by modulating his voice, by every movement of hands and body, wanted them to know that he *resented* them having to be here. Subliminally he was telling them that the defendant didn't so much as deserve a trial, that she was guilty as hell, and what was to come was simply confirmation of that irrefutable fact.

It took a brilliant lawyer to make it work. Garrett, while not brilliant, was smart and cunning, and he was showing those skills now.

"Andrew Marsh made what turned out to be a fatal mistake," he began. "He fell in love."

He paused for effect, then said, "He fell in love with a ruthless, calculating woman who went after an elderly man with a bad heart and a big bank account."

He pointed at Rebecca. Prosecutors loved to do that, point at the defendant. It had become a cliché, but they did it anyway, because it worked. They hoped the jury would see it as sign that the accusation was backed by the force of truth.

Frank could feel his own heart pounding. Out of the corner of his eye he stole a glance at his client, sitting there coolly, her jaw thrust forward, looking serene and confident, unwilting under the combined stare of everyone in the courtroom following the path of Garrett's finger.

Frank had coached her on the pointed finger, told her it would happen. And she'd listened. Too bad about the clothes and makeup. He wished she'd listened to him on that point as well. For now, with her blond hair and tight dress, she seemed to emphasize the very characteristics Garrett was trying to exploit.

Garrett was still pointing, making this a big production. "You all can see the defendant, Rebecca Carlson. But as this trial proceeds you will see that she is not only the defendant . . . she is the murder weapon itself."

He finally dropped the extended arm, then put his hand to his chin, as if thinking. He lifted his head and said, "Is that possible? Can a person actually be a weapon?"

He provided his own answer. "The answer is yes.

"If I hit you and you die . . . I am the cause of your death. But can I be called a weapon? Yes. And what a deadly weapon Rebecca Carlson made of it.

"The state will prove that she seduced Andrew Marsh and manipulated his affections until he rewrote his will . . . leaving her ten . . . million dollars."

The spectators mumbled. It was a hell of a motive.

Garrett paused again, then said, "That she insisted on increasingly strenuous sex . . . knowing he had a severe heart condition. And when that didn't work fast enough for her? She secretly doped him with cocaine! His heart couldn't take the combination, and she got what she wanted."

He waited for his words to sink in.

"She is a beautiful woman . . . but when this trial is over, you will see her no differently than a gun or a knife or any other instrument used as a weapon.

"She is a killer. And the worst kind . . . a killer who disguised herself as a loving partner."

Garrett gripped the edge of the table, waited a moment, then took his seat.

The judge looked at Frank. "Mr. Dulaney?"

Frank shuffled some papers, then stood and faced the jury. He stuffed his hands in his pockets to appear casual as he walked slowly toward them. Then he took his hands out of his pockets and let his arms fall by his side.

"Ladies and gentlemen . . . you were told during jury selection that the testimony in this trial would be sexually explicit. And you may find it offensive. You may even be disgusted by what you hear."

He lowered his head, rubbed his chin, then looked at them, his expression friendly and sincere, the tone of his voice even and calm. "But Rebecca Carlson is not on trial for her sexual tastes," he said. "You must understand that if you are to render a fair verdict in this case."

He straightened up and raised his voice as he said, "She's being tried for murder! And to charge her with murder is ludicrous."

He looked at Garrett for a moment, then back at the jurors, making eye contact with each one in turn as he spoke.

"The state would like you to believe that she somehow *fornicated* Andrew Marsh to death."

He let that sink in, too.

"But the state's case is based on fantasy, not fact. And the facts, such as they are, are entirely circumstantial. It isn't a crime to be a beautiful woman! It isn't a crime to fall in love with an older man! This case should never have come to trial."

He leaned forward, wanting their full attention. He was getting it.

"But since it has," he said, "I know that when you listen to the testimony . . . objectively . . . and when you hear the evidence . . . *objectively* . . . you'll acquit Rebecca Carlson of the charges against her."

Frank thanked the jurors, noted their expressions, then sat down. He was pleased. The jurors appeared to be trying hard not to be influenced either way at this point. They seemed to be saying they would listen to the evidence and then decide. The first hurdle had been successfully jumped.

Frank tried to steal a quick glance at Rebecca to see how she was holding up. She saw him and held his attention with a look that startled him.

It was a look of pure veneration.

He felt a shiver go through him.

Garrett's first witnesses were a couple of cops. Nothing much there. They talked about being called to the house, finding Marsh, and contacting the medical examiner's office.

Then Garrett called the ME to the stand. Dr. McCurdy was an old hand at murder trials and looked almost bored as he took his seat in the witness stand. Garrett asked him a few innocuous questions, then got to the main thrust of his inquiry.

"Doctor, can you tell us what you found when you performed an autopsy on the body of Andrew Marsh?"

"Yes. I found a high concentration of cocaine in the blood of the deceased. Combined with his preexisting heart disease and the sexual activity that he evidenced at the scene, the drug overstimulated his heart muscle and produced a major ventricular arrhythmia leading to cardiac arrest."

"A heart attack, in other words."

"Yes."

"Dr. McCurdy, did you find any indication that Mr. Marsh might have used cocaine on a regular basis?"

McCurdy started shaking his head before Garrett had even finished asking the question. "No," he said. "His nasal membranes were way too smooth for even occasional use."

"Were you able to determine how he ingested the drug?"

"A bottle of nasal spray found next to the bed was filled with a mixture of water and cocaine. The victim had a head cold at the time of his death. I believe he was drugged without his knowledge."

"Objection," Frank interjected, raising his arm in the air. "Lack of foundation. The witness is speculating. Motion to strike the testimony, Your Honor."

"So ordered," the judge said quickly. She looked at the jury box and added, "The jury will disregard the witness's comment."

Easy to say, hard to do, Frank thought. As in all criminal trials, juries remembered what they wanted to remember. Admonishments rarely had much effect, and everyone knew it. It was the reason that prosecutors often mentioned inadmissible evidence or introduced unacceptable testimony early in the proceedings.

The jury would always be instructed to disregard, but the images remained, the words etched in memory banks. Too many admonishments from a judge could be cause for a mistrial. Most experienced lawyers would take it to the limit, but stop short of going too far.

Already, Robert Garrett was testing the judicial waters, sticking in his big toe, then pulling it back. Score one for the prosecutor.

Garrett removed a bottle of nasal spray from an evidence bag and held it up. "Was this the spray you found, Doctor?"

McCurdy looked at the bottle, then said, "Yes, it was."

Garrett looked up at the judge. "Introduced as People's Exhibit A."

The judge nodded and made a note. The court clerk made an entry as well.

"And," Garrett continued, addressing McCurdy, "what would cocaine do to someone in Mr. Marsh's condition?"

Dr. McCurdy brushed some lint from his sleeve and said laconically, "Accelerate his heartbeat."

Garrett's eyebrows arched. "And if he

were having sex while under the influence of such a stimulant?"

The doctor hesitated for a moment, then said, "It would be the same as shooting a loaded gun at him."

Frank knew that this was an outrageous analogy. He wanted to object, but experience told him not to. Judges disliked constant interruption, as did juries. Since the words had already registered with the jury and the judge would probably allow them to stand, Frank held his tongue.

Garrett picked up a folder, a thin smile on his lips, and began to read. "You said in your autopsy report that Mr. Marsh was restrained at the time of his death. Would you explain that, please?"

Frank couldn't allow that one to pass unchallenged. He leaped to his feet, his hand raised again. "Objection. The prosecution is trying to introduce inflammatory, irrelevant testimony."

"Your Honor," Garrett protested, both arms extended, his hands palms up, "the jury has a right to know the circumstances of the victim's death!"

Judge Burnham glowered, then beckoned both lawyers to the bench. Her long, red nails seemed like claws.

As they stood at the bench the judge

frowned, leaned forward, and glared at Garrett. "Are you testing me already, Mr. Garrett?"

"No, ma'am," Garrett replied, looking almost helpless. "If an autopsy report qualifies as titillation, I can't control that."

She thought for a moment, then said, "Watch yourselves, both of you."

Then, so everyone could hear, she announced, "The objection's overruled."

She turned to Dr. McCurdy. "You may answer the question, Doctor."

McCurdy faced Garrett and said, "From the marks on his wrists and the marks on the bedstead, I believe the victim was handcuffed."

That got the spectators mumbling again.

"At the time of his death?" Garrett asked, pushing hard.

"Oh, yes. The friction and bruising was extensive. He was struggling."

Garrett looked like the cat that had swallowed the canary. "Thank you, Dr. McCurdy."

He turned away from the witness and smiled at Frank. "Your witness."

Frank got to his feet and stood near the witness box, his arms crossed over his chest. "Doctor, you testified that in your opinion Mr. Marsh suffered his fatal heart attack while he was restrained."

"Yes, sir."

"And your evidence for that was the marks on his wrists, am I right?"

"Yes, you are."

"Couldn't those same marks have been made while he was"—Frank started waving his arms around like a man trying to fly—"flailing around in the throes of sexual ecstasy?"

The doctor frowned, thought for a moment, then said, "I suppose."

Frank looked incredulous. "Did you find any older marks that indicated use of restraints?"

"Just on his ankles."

"Where they wouldn't show in public . . ."

Garrett leaped to his feet. "Objection. Counsel's drawing his own conclusion."

"Sustained," Judge Burnham intoned. "You know better, Frank."

Frank gave her a nod, then said, "Let me rephrase. Did the marks indicate to you that Mr. Marsh played bondage games on a regular basis?"

"Objection," Garrett protested, still on his feet. "Counsel's asking for a personal opinion."

"Sustained."

Frank took note of the increased heat in

the judge's voice. He was still within a margin of safety. "Doctor, can you medically say that Mr. Marsh didn't *decide* to get high?"

Garrett finally took his seat.

"It seems very unlikely that a man with his set of conditions—"

Frank cut him off with a wave of the hand. "Are you a licensed psychiatrist, Dr. McCurdy?"

"No, but . . ."

Garrett was on his feet again. "Objection! Argumentative."

Frank, in full view of the jury, made a face, the face of a man truly astounded by such a silly objection. Judge Burnham saw the ploy for what it was and increased her irritation level two full notches. "Sustained," she bellowed.

Now Frank *was* in the danger zone. Time to watch out. He turned and faced Rebecca, giving her a small smile. She returned it, and it seemed as if a light had been switched on in the room.

Frank turned back to face the witness. "How did you reach your conclusion about what Mr. Marsh would or wouldn't do?" he asked.

The question was designed to be impossible to answer. McCurdy's response was predictable. "Common sense . . ."

"Did you find any evidence of that in the autopsy?" Frank asked. Then, without waiting for an answer: "Do you know for a fact that Andrew Marsh *had* any common sense? Didn't you just testify that he *liked* unpleasant things?"

"Your Honor," Garrett pleaded, half rising, that helpless look back on his face.

Frank raised his palms in surrender, smiled, then said, "No more questions."

Judge Burnham wasn't going to let him off that easily. For all to hear, she said, "It's going to be a long trial for you, counselor, if I have to start warning you on the first day."

Frank hung his head for a moment, then apologized. But when he took his seat, he sat straight, a look of confidence on his face. He knew he'd blunted some of the effect of McCurdy's testimony. Not all, but some.

He felt Rebecca's presence next to him, the scent of her perfume wafting through the air. When he turned and looked at her, her eyes expressed her appreciation. He was her champion, she seemed to be saying. He was going to save her from the clutches of these cretins. His skill and his dedication would win out. He could see she had full confidence in him.

And when she reached out and touched his hand, it was as if he'd stuck his finger in a light socket.

During the afternoon recess, Frank and Rebecca were closeted in one of the small client/lawyer conference rooms adjacent to the courtroom, taking a slight respite from the fierce intensity of the trial.

"How are we doing?" Rebecca asked.

"It's just begun," he said, "but it's going well. They have no case. Andrew Marsh died of a heart attack. It wasn't your fault, pure and simple."

She took his hand in hers and squeezed it. "Are you still angry with me?" she asked.

"For what?"

"For not dressing like an old maid?"

She was smiling, teasing him gently. He shrugged. "It would have helped," he said. "I don't think you realize the impact you have on people."

She smiled. "Maybe not. I thought your opening statement was wonderful."

"Thank you."

"You really *do* believe in me, don't you?"

He looked at her for a moment, then said, "Let me put it this way, Rebecca. Even if you were an ax murderer, with bodies found all over the city and your prints on the ax. Maybe even photographs of you doing the deeds . . . you're still entitled to the best defense I can muster.

"This isn't about guilt or innocence. This is about you getting a fair trial. I'm going to make sure that happens."

The smile dropped from her lips. She looked hurt. "So, what you're really saying is that you think I did it."

Frank waved a hand in the air. "I didn't say that at all. It doesn't matter what I think."

"Maybe not to you, but it does to me."

"It's a little late," he said.

"Why won't you tell me?" she insisted.

"Why won't you wear the clothes I asked you to?" he countered.

Again, she smiled, but he could see her lips trembling slightly.

"Okay," he said. "If you really want to know—"

She tensed.

"I think you're innocent," he said.

The tension drained from her. Now she glowed.

There was a rap at the door. "Two minutes," the bailiff said.

◆ ◆ ◆

Back in court, Garrett put Dr. Steven Trammel, Andrew Marsh's cardiologist, on the stand. The doctor was a thin, pasty-faced man in his fifties, who lacked the presence of the experienced medical examiner. He appeared nervous, crossing his legs first one way and then the other.

"Dr. Trammel," Garrett began, "when did you first diagnose that Andrew Marsh had heart disease?"

Dr. Trammel took a deep breath, then said, "A year and a half ago, according to my records."

"Did Rebecca Carlson ever accompany Mr. Marsh to your office?"

The doctor glanced furtively at Rebecca, then said, "Yes, she did once."

Garrett nodded, then asked, "What does the sign on your office door say?"

The doctor blinked, then said, "Dr. Steven Trammel, Cardiologist."

Garrett smiled, turned away from the witness and waved a hand at Frank. His turn.

Frank stood up. "Dr. Trammel," he said, "did you ever discuss Marsh's health with Rebecca?"

"No."

"Did you ever discuss it in *front* of Rebecca?"

"No."

"Did she ever go into the examining room with him?"

There was a pause, then: "No."

"Then you have no indication that she knew how serious his condition was, do you?"

"Not really."

Frank suppressed a smile. "Does 'not really' mean 'no'?"

"I don't know what she knew," he answered.

"Thank you, Doctor."

Frank started to sit, then straightened up again, as though he had an afterthought. It wasn't an afterthought at all. The strategy was written into his notes.

"Um . . . one last question, please. Do you know why Mr. Marsh brought Rebecca with him to your office?"

"He wanted me to buy some photographs from her," the doctor answered, his face flushed with embarrassment.

Garrett, trying to draw attention away from the question, sank slightly in his chair and laced his hands over his belly. It drew a smile from Frank. He turned back to the doctor, the smile still fixed on his lips. "Did you buy any?"

The doctor's blush deepened. "They were too expensive," he explained.

Some of the spectators laughed. Frank caught Rebecca looking at him, the look of admiration strong on her face. She was beaming at him, building a fire within him. He almost strutted back to the table. "No more questions," he said, his eyes fixed on Rebecca.

Garrett called another doctor to the stand. Alan Paley was a serious-faced man of about thirty, who seemed even more ill at ease than the previous witness.

Paley's slightly bulging eyes moved jerkily within their sockets as first he looked at Garrett, then at Frank, then Rebecca, and back to Garrett. He fidgeted in the chair, his hand playing with the knot on his tie, then falling away, only to return. His thin lips opened and closed as his nostrils flared.

"Where do you work, Dr. Paley?" Garrett asked.

Paley's hand went to the tie again. "I'm an emergency-room physician at Memorial Hospital."

"Were you on duty the night of February fifth this year?"

"I was the admitting physician . . . yes, I was."

Garrett's voice level went up a notch. He was leading to something important. "Did you admit Andrew Marsh to the hospital that night?"

Paley gulped, then said, "Yes, I did."

"What was the reason?"

"Cocaine poisoning," the doctor said, his gaze falling on Rebecca. Quickly he brought his attention back to Garrett.

"Did Mr. Marsh discuss the circumstances with you?" Garrett asked.

The doctor swallowed hard, then cleared his throat. His obvious nervousness was making him a very sympathetic witness.

Here was an emergency-room doctor, dedicated to saving lives, being forced to testify in one of the most sensational trials in Portland history. Clearly he was out of his element, and it showed. He was trained and conditioned to act, not to sit in a chair in front of scores of strangers and answer questions.

"Uh . . . yes, he did," he said. "I read my notes again before I came, to be accurate, and according to my notes the patient told me that it was the first time he'd tried cocaine and it was going to be the last."

Frank felt another adrenaline surge. Dr. Paley's name was on the witness list provided by Garrett prior to the start of the trial, as required by law. But when Frank had interviewed the man, the doctor had contended that Marsh's trip to the emergency room was because of a heart problem. The doctor had never mentioned cocaine, nor was cocaine mentioned in the hospital records.

Not mentioning cocaine in the official hospital records was not that unusual. Andrew Marsh was a wealthy and influential man, one capable of making sure there was no record of him committing a possible felony. Hospitals often fudged the records of the wealthy for their protection.

But for the doctor to omit reference to cocaine during Frank's taking of his deposition was something else again. Marsh was already dead. He couldn't hurt the doctor.

Had Frank failed to elicit this testimony from the doctor during the deposition? Had he written the doctor off as an unimportant witness, thereby allowing him to escape the questions being asked now?

That wasn't like Frank. Usually his depositions were thorough and pointed. But there was no escaping the fact that he'd missed this.

He was steaming inside, angry with himself for screwing up. First, there'd been the delay in getting the deposition from Joanne Braslow, a deposition that was most damaging to Rebecca. Garrett had set Frank up with that one, and Frank had let him get away with it.

Now Garrett was bringing forth testimony from a witness that was just as damaging, testimony that Frank should have drawn out during the deposition. Frank was being sabotaged by his own sudden incompetence.

Garrett was now warming to his task, speaking clearly, making sure the jury heard every word. "Would you describe his heart condition, please?"

"He presented a galaxy of symptoms," Paley said. "Hyperpyrexia, which is a high fever associated with cocaine intoxication . . . severely elevated blood pressure . . . arrhythmia . . . shortness of breath . . . and while I was examining the patient, he experienced status epilepticus, a specific type of convulsion."

"Is it common to have that many symptoms occur in cases of cocaine poisoning?"

Paley swallowed hard again. "This patient was particularly sensitive," he said. "I thought he was lucky to go home alive."

Garrett leaned forward, a smile on his lips. "Did you tell him that, Dr. Paley?"

Paley thought for a moment, then said, "I don't remember if I used those exact words, but he fully understood his intolerance to the drug."

Garrett turned and faced Frank, a look of triumph on his face. "Your witness."

Frank was completely unprepared. He'd been operating under a false assumption. He looked at Rebecca. With her eyes, she signaled that she could be of no help. There was nothing Frank could do but let it pass as if the testimony was meaningless. He needed time to think.

He made a big play of examining some papers, then looked up at the judge and said, "No questions for this witness, Your Honor."

Even Garrett seemed surprised.

Frank's sense of uneasiness took a quantum leap.


The next witness called by the prosecution was Joanne Braslow. As before, she was dressed conservatively, looking almost mousy, her face devoid of makeup, her hair combed but not styled. She looked like a prissy schoolmarm.

As usual, Garrett started his examination in a relaxed manner, letting the witness get comfortable in a foreign setting. Then, sensing that the witness was ready, he started throwing the hardball questions.

"Did you see Mr. Marsh the day before his death, Miss Braslow?"

Joanne shifted in the chair, then said, "Yes."

"How did he look?"

Her eyes seemed to mist. "He was pale and sweating."

"Did you talk about Miss Carlson?"

At the mention of Rebecca's name, the hardness returned to Joanne's face. "Yes," she said.

"What did he say?"

"He was worried," she said. "*I* was worried. He said that if she kept it up, she was going to kill him." A pause. "His heart couldn't take it," she added.

The crowd started buzzing. Rebecca seemed stunned, her head lowered, her eyes focused on the table in front of her. She looked pale.

Frank leaned toward her and whispered in her ear. "Take it easy," he said. "I warned you this testimony would come in. You can't let it bother you. And even if it does, you can't let them see your reaction. Okay?"

Rebecca nodded, gripped his hand, then lifted her head. She was trying, but her eyes were the eyes of a frightened doe caught in the sights of a hunter's rifle.

Garrett was finished with the witness.

Frank stood up, nodded to Garrett, then approached the witness. "Miss Braslow," he said, a note of incredulity in his voice, "this strikes me as a very intimate conversation for a boss to have with his secretary. Did you often discuss his love life?"

Her lips tightened for a moment. Then she said, "We had a professional relationship, but I'd been his secretary for six years. He liked to talk to me."

Frank smiled. "Then did he also tell you that Rebecca was thinking about moving back to Chicago?"

A pause, then: "Yes . . . he mentioned it."

"So the woman he loved passionately was thinking about leaving. Couldn't *that* have caused the anxiety and stress you observed?"

Garrett objected immediately. Raising his arm, he shouted, "This calls for rank speculation, Your Honor."

Frank was ready. He took two steps toward the bench and said, "Counsel for the prosecution has already used this witness to establish the state of mind of the deceased. He opened the can, Your Honor."

Judge Burnham gave Garrett a sharp retort. "And I do see worms crawling all around you, Mr. Garrett. You can't have it both ways. Objection overruled. Answer the question, Miss Braslow."

Now it was Joanne who looked like a frightened doe. "He never said he loved her," she said weakly.

Frank pounced on the answer. "That wasn't the question," he hissed. "I asked if the possibility of losing her could have caused the anxiety and stress you observed. That if she *left,* it would kill him because he couldn't live *without* her? That his heart couldn't take a breakup?"

Garrett jumped to his feet objecting, but his heart wasn't really in it. The objection was more to impress the jury, and the judge knew it. She waved him back down, then said "Overruled" for the record.

Frank was staring at the witness, making eye contact, his brooding eyes boring holes into her skull. "Think about it, Joanne. Isn't it possible?"

Garrett was still trying, on his feet again. Judge Burnham was becoming irritated. "Overruled," she shouted.

Frank waited impatiently. Finally Joanne reluctantly acceded. "I suppose it's possible."

Frank turned and went back to his table, more to give the jury time to absorb

Joanne's words than anything else. He slyly winked at Rebecca before facing the witness again, his confidence returning with a rush.

"Now," he said to Joanne, his voice strong and sure, "you testified that you saw Rebecca inhaling cocaine in the bathroom. How did you know it was cocaine?"

Joanne was clearly upset. She was a woman who didn't appreciate having her words questioned. "It was a white powder, all right?"

Another weak answer. Frank waited for a moment, looked at the jurors, then sprang the question he'd been wanting to ask from the start. "Have you ever been a patient at a rehab center? A rehabilitation center?"

Joanne's eyes bulged and her mouth dropped open. Garrett leaped to his feet, face flushed, hands gesticulating, mouth in overdrive.

"Objection!" he screamed. "Miss Braslow's medical history has no bearing—"

Frank cut him off. "Your Honor, the prosecution has introduced cocaine as one of the contributing causes of death! This is a reasonable line of questioning."

"I'll allow it," the judge said firmly.

Garrett, stunned, took his seat, looking almost as upset as the witness. Frank, after making a big deal of checking his notes again, resumed the attack.

"Were you a patient at a rehabilitation center from January fifth to February fifth two years ago?" he asked Joanne.

She looked pale, her chest heaving as she fought for air. For a moment her eyes jerked about the room, as if someone would announce that she need not answer the question. But there was no escape.

"Yes," she said, humiliated, her voice barely audible.

Now Frank had the look of triumph. "What were you being treated for?"

It was sheer agony for her to utter the words. "Substance and alcohol abuse."

"Was the substance cocaine?"

She hesitated, then: "Yes."

"And didn't you supply your boss, Mr. Marsh, with the cocaine that sent him to the hospital with cocaine poisoning last year?"

"No," she shouted.

Frank pulled a document from his briefcase. Standing in front of the witness box, he said, "I have in my hand a copy of the admissions report the night Mr. Marsh was admitted."

She stiffened, dreading what was coming next. Frank walked slowly to the witness stand and handed her the document. Then he said, "In the square right here designated for the signature of the responsible party, the person who brought him to the hospital . . . would you please read the name out loud?"

Joanne looked physically ill.

"Read the name out loud, please!" Frank insisted.

Joanne looked at the document, then turned away. In almost a whisper, she said, "Joanne Braslow, but—"

"No further questions," Frank said, cutting her off. He then turned to the judge. "Your Honor, I submit Defense Exhibit A."

Frank walked over to Garrett, handing him the document. Garrett, red-faced and angry, looked ready to commit murder himself.

Frank took the document back and looked at it closely. He hadn't missed it, as he feared. The word *cocaine* did not appear anywhere on the hospital admissions record of Andrew Marsh.

It was a relief, but it still didn't explain his error in not dragging it out of Paley during the deposition.

Court was adjourned for the day.

The sound of people rushing for the door reverberated through the courtroom. The buzz of conversation reached a crescendo, then began to fade.

Garrett left without so much as a glance at Frank. But Rebecca was staring at him, her eyes aglow, the look of admiration strong and penetrating.

"You were marvelous," she said, wrapping her arms around him in a strong hug.

"Thank you," he said, gently extricating himself. He held her elbows in his hands. "For an opening day, it wasn't too bad at all."

Rebecca's touch seemed to electrify him. It was disconcerting, but he didn't want to break the contact. He saw Gabe grinning at him, the same admiration expressed in his eyes.

"Gabe," Frank said, "I need to go over some things with you."

"Sure."

Frank turned to Rebecca. "This may take some time," he said. Then, impulsively, he added, "Why don't we discuss things over dinner tonight?"

She ran her tongue over her lips. "That's a wonderful idea," she said.

He felt a shiver go down his spine.

"I'll pick you up. Say eight?"

Her eyes gleamed. "Eight will be fine."

"Great," he said. And as he picked up his briefcase he noticed his hand was trembling.

8

◆Frank felt buoyed, exhilarated, in the mood to celebrate. He took her to one of Portland's better restaurants in the Skidmore Historic District, where the food was excellent and the prices reflected it. The hell with it. A celebration was a celebration.

As they drove from her houseboat to the restaurant, he kept up a steady patter, explaining the intricacies of some of the testimony and courtroom procedures.

But his mind was elsewhere.

She was dressed in a simple black dress with a scoop neck that exposed the top portion of her breasts. She carried a thin cloth coat over her arm. Her hair was down again, a mass of soft curls and waves. Her face shone in the yellow light cast by cars passing in the other direction.

When they reached the office building

housing the restaurant, he left the car with the valet and took her arm. The night air was cool and damp, almost foggy, the street lamps glimmering through the moisture.

Together, they walked down the curved staircase leading to the restaurant.

The hostess recognized them immediately, and her eyes widened in shock. She couldn't speak.

Rebecca was suddenly reticent. She pulled at Frank's arm, saying, "You picked a very public place, Frank."

"That's the point," he replied. "You're an innocent woman with nothing to hide."

A few of the customers seated nearest the entrance spotted them and stared unabashedly at Rebecca. The men were gawking, while the women's faces held expressions of disgust.

"Reservation for Dulaney," Frank said confidently to the hostess.

She was too intimidated to respond. She simply led them to their table.

As they passed other tables there were more stares, and a few whispered remarks. One of the men locked eyes with Frank, then looked quickly away.

They took their seats. Rebecca seemed oblivious to the stares, focusing her attention on Frank. The idea had been to talk business, but business was quickly forgotten. Frank realized he just wanted to be with her. Pure and simple.

Frank picked up a linen table napkin and placed it across his lap. Then he picked up the menu. "What do you prefer?" he asked Rebecca.

"Why don't you order for us both?" she said, a lilt in her voice.

"You sure?"

"I like everything," she said softly. "You should know that by now."

He almost dropped the menu.

He ordered squab with wild rice and assorted vegetables, all simmered in a delicious combination of herbs and spices, accompanied by a '71 Château Lafite. It was an outrageous extravagance, absolutely frivolous, but he was wired. The wine did little to bring him down.

Nor did Rebecca. Over coffee, she leaned back in her chair, totally relaxed, and said, "I love watching you in court. Did you always want to be a lawyer?"

Frank smiled. "It was my fallback. I was going to play pro hockey."

"What happened?"

"I broke my ankle skating. I was showing off."

She clucked her tongue. "How old were you?"

"Seven."

"You lived here?"

"Yes. I like it here. Portland is my favorite city."

"Have you ever lived anywhere else?"

"No."

"Then how do you know?"

He laughed. "You sound like a lawyer. Actually I've been to quite a few cities. But nothing compares to this one. It's different here, maybe because the city is big enough to have some great attractions, but not so big as to have all the problems associated with bigger cities.

"I like the river. I like the mountains. I like the nearness of the ocean. On a good day, it's only an hour and a half away. If I had to pick a dislike, I'd pick the weather, but what the hell.

"But most of all, I like the people. They're solid, decent people, warm and friendly most of the time. Nice to be around."

"Decent," she repeated, an edge to her voice.

He blushed. "That wasn't a reflection on you," he said quickly.

She put the smile back on her face, then

slowly licked her lips. "I know," she said.

Frank blushed again.

She laughed at his discomfort, and then her eyes became wistful. "When I was seven," she said, "I liked to steal strawberries. I used to sneak into the yard at the end of the street. There was a tall fence. It wasn't easy. I'd scrape my knees just climbing over it. Then on the other side were these wild rosebushes. The thorns would dig into my legs and cut my thighs as I slid down. But the strawberries were always so sweet."

"Because of how much it hurt to get them," Frank noted.

She smiled provocatively. "I think you're beginning to understand me, Frank."

"Perhaps I am," he said.

"And what do you see?"

He sipped his coffee, then put the cup down. "I see a woman falsely accused of murder."

She licked her lips again. "You know what I mean."

"I see a woman who likes to play rough," he said. "I see a survivor, a woman with tremendous strength, a woman willing to do what it takes to get what she wants."

Her eyebrows arched. "Is that bad?"

He shook his head. "Not at all, within

certain limits. Men have been acting this way since day one. It's hard to fault a woman for doing it."

She lowered her head slightly and looked at him through her long lashes. "The limits you mentioned. What exactly are they?"

"The same limits that apply to everyone," he said.

"You mean the legal limits."

"Yes."

She smiled, tossed her head back, and took a deep breath. Then she leaned forward, her arms pressed close to her sides, almost forcing her breasts out of the dress.

Frank stared.

"You're still a little unsure, aren't you?"

"About what?" he said.

"About Andrew. There's still some doubt in your mind."

He finally pulled his gaze away from her chest. "No. There's no doubt. I know you didn't do it."

She reached forward and touched his hand.

He cleared his throat. "How'd you know when you met Marsh that he was, well, like you?"

His eyes suddenly seemed out of focus. He could feel his heart pounding inside his rib cage. Her grip on his hand tightened.

"There was a party," she said, remembering. "It was a big crowd, but we saw each other." A pause. "And we knew."

"Just like that?"

"You can tell," she said, her eyes lustful.

She slowly removed her hand. His seemed to be on fire.

He was fascinated. He'd never indulged in sadomasochism, either before marriage or after. To him, it made no sense.

And yet, sitting in close proximity to a woman who relished it, he found himself intensely curious, desire strong within him, and it was because of Rebecca. She was awakening emotions he never knew existed, and the unfamiliar experience almost took his breath away.

"Okay," he said to Rebecca. "Look around."

She knew exactly what he meant. "You want to know if there's anybody in the restaurant who has the same tastes I do?"

"Sure," he said.

She took a moment. "Let's see." Then she slowly looked around the room. People who stared at her dropped their gazes as her eyes met theirs. She took her time, capturing the entire room and everyone in it, then turned her attention back to Frank.

"All right," he said. "Who?"

"I'm not going to tell you," she said coquettishly.

"Why not?"

Her eyes were magnetic, holding him fast, her gaze reaching deep inside his soul.

"Because he doesn't know yet," she said.

A shiver went up his spine.

With a sense of expectation, Frank drove Rebecca home. As they walked along the dock toward her houseboat, even the air seemed alive, heavy with moisture, glowing in the reflected light of the moon. The wooden slats creaked beneath their feet as the water slapped softly against the wooden pilings.

The faint sound of a television-show laugh track drifted out from one of the other houseboats.

Rebecca was holding his arm, looking up at the stars flickering in the night sky, completely at peace. She turned and looked at Frank, her eyes shimmering in the moonlight. "Yes . . . it would be nice," she said softly.

"What would?" Frank asked.

"You and I making love."

He felt a surge of adrenaline. "Is that

what you think I was thinking?"

They reached the door to her houseboat. She stood there, looking up at him, the smell of her filling his nostrils. She was offering herself to him and he wanted her badly, but something held him back. He was speechless.

She squeezed his arm. "There's nothing wrong with admitting that you want me, Frank."

She was teasing him, her mouth open, her head tilted back, her eyes slightly hooded, the embodiment of sexuality. His head moved toward her involuntarily. Closer. Inches away. He could almost feel the softness of her lips on his, taste the delicious sweetness.

"You take a lot for granted," he said, his voice barely above a whisper.

He felt her hand on his chest, stopping him.

"Frank—"

He pulled back. Rebecca shrugged apologetically, her eyes suddenly indifferent. "Go home," she said. "Thanks for dinner."

In one quick move she was gone. She left him standing there, shutting the door in his face. For a moment he stood rooted, then spun around and walked away, his hands jammed in his pockets, feeling humiliated, feeling like the fool again, his confidence shattered.

She'd toyed with him. She'd made it obvious she wanted him and he'd responded in kind. Then, proving her power over him, she'd pushed him away. That was bad enough, but what was worse was the fact that he was ready to make love to her at all.

Jesus. What if Sharon had found out? What in hell had he been thinking of?

He strode purposefully down the dock and up to the street, and then to his car. But before he got in, his eyes were drawn back to the houseboat. He could see the curtains upstairs fluttering in the gentle breeze, the weak, shadowy light behind them flickering eerily.

He got into the car and closed the door, determined to put her out of his mind. But something within him made him look again; at the flickering light inside the houseboat—the light in Rebecca's bedroom.

He knew. They were flickering candles, acting like beacons, not warning him away, but calling to him. Just part of the game Rebecca wanted to play.

He shoved the key in the ignition. He had to get out of there and go home. This was crazy, dangerous and stupid. She was simply playing with him, tweaking his emotions, and if he caved in to her, she'd probably laugh in his face.

Again, he turned and looked at the houseboat.

He saw her on the balcony, carrying a bottle of champagne by the neck. She raised it slowly, then wrapped her lips around its mouth and took a long swallow. Then she slowly brought the bottle down and leaned on the rail, her arms crossed, her hair moving with the breeze, her body primed and waiting.

His heart started pounding wildly. It was crazy, he knew, but he wanted her terribly. Being made a fool of meant nothing. Having her meant everything. At the moment it was all he could think about.

Suddenly he was galvanized, his entire being focused on the shadowy figure on the houseboat. He pulled the key from the ignition and bolted out of the car, his long legs taking him quickly back to the dock, to the houseboat—and Rebecca.

He reached the door and stopped. Perhaps it was locked. Perhaps he was imagining things. Perhaps—

She opened the door before his hand touched the knob.

No words were spoken. Like two hawks,

Rebecca Lawson (Madonna) and Frank Dulaney (Willem Dafoe) facing their attraction.

Rebecca Lawson (Madonna) mourns for Andrew Marsh.

Anne Archer as Andrew Marsh's secretary Joanne Braslow.

Willem Dafoe as successful, well-respected criminal defense attorney Frank Dulaney.

Assistant District Attorney Robert Garrett as played by Joe Mantegna.

Jurgen Prochnow as Dr. Alan Paley.

Stan Shaw as Charles Biggs, investigator for the defense.

The Dulaneys share a happy time. *From left:* Sharon Dulaney (Julianne Moore), Michael Dulaney (Aaron Corcoran) and Frank Dulaney (Willem Dafoe).

A marked man. Frank Dulaney as played by Willem Dafoe.

The truth begins to unwind. Frank (Willem Dafoe) and Biggs (Stan Shaw) view the videotape.

Frank (Willem Dafoe) tries to win Sharon (Julianne Moore) back.

Rebecca (Madonna) tells Frank (Willem Dafoe) the truth.

Alan Paley (Jurgen Prochnow) and Rebecca (Madonna) admit their deception.

they clutched and clawed at each other, tearing at each other's clothes as they made their way toward the stairs, then up them, half crawling, half pulling, moaning, groaning, consumed with passion.

His heart seemed about to burst. He gasped for air, groaned, then finally tasted that marvelous mouth. Her tongue darted inside his mouth and explored deeply. He did the same. She took it in her mouth and sucked hard while her hand grabbed his crotch and found his hardness.

They stumbled into the bedroom, panting and moaning, their faces flushed with emotion, their eyes gleaming with passion. The light of a half-dozen candles cast a flickering light across Rebecca's marvelous skin.

Quickly she unhooked her bra, and her full breasts spilled out into his hands. He bent forward, forcing her to lean backward, then lifted her to him.

His mouth covered a hard nipple, which he sucked urgently. Then he did the same with the other. He was on fire, the blood pounding in his temples, setting off little bursts of light behind his eyes.

They fell to the bed. Rebecca pushed her panties off her legs and kicked them to the floor. The sight of her nakedness drove him wild. He leaned forward and pressed his mouth between her legs, his tongue probing, darting in and out, his teeth pulling at her pubic hair.

She pulled away from him, her mouth open, her eyes glazed, her breath coming in short bursts. She unzipped his fly and exposed his throbbing penis. Her hands cupped his testicles as she took his penis in her mouth. Then, suddenly, she tightened her grip. He cried out in pain.

She released him immediately and threw herself back on the bed, spreading her legs and arching her pelvis invitingly.

He was almost out of his mind with desire. He drove himself inside her. He could feel her bare heel digging into his back, urging him on.

He needed no urging.

And then, suddenly, she rolled out from under him, coming up behind him, pressing her naked body against him, her expert, probing hands finding his flesh again.

She unbuckled his belt. He lifted his hips to help. In one swift move she whipped the belt out of the loops, around his elbows, through the wrought-iron headboard, and almost before he knew it, he found himself hauled into a half-sitting position, his arms tied firmly to the head-board.

Suddenly he was afraid. He bucked to pull himself free, but the belt held.

He was her prisoner.

Rebecca, her eyes glistening in the light, leaned forward and kissed him hard, her teeth biting at his lower lip. She brushed her nipples against his.

"Are you scared?" she asked tauntingly.

"No," he lied.

In truth, he was terrified, but he was damned if he'd admit it. But her eyes told him she knew. She could see right through his bluster, to the man beneath the facade, the man both terrified and inflamed with unfamiliar and unconventional yearning.

Slowly she removed his socks, then his trousers, and finally his shorts. She heaped his clothes in a neat little pile on the floor, then leaned forward and took one testicle in her mouth.

He moaned.

She was an expert, applying just enough mouth pressure to bring him to the edge of pain, but not enough to dim his ardor. First one, and then the other.

She was in her element, completely in control, and her every move reflected the satisfaction she got from domination. Her eyes gleamed, her skin glowed with perspiration, and her breasts heaved with every gasp of air.

She straddled him and knelt, moving her hips in tight small circles. He could feel her pubic hair brushing his, feel her hot wetness caressing his stomach. And when she rubbed the tip of his penis against her labia, the fear began to dissipate as raw desire took its place.

"You're not in charge," she said, her voice husky now, lower than normal. "You've got nothing to worry about. You don't have to do anything. You *can't*."

She reached for one of the candles and the bottle of champagne. Fear flickered afresh in Frank's eyes. She saw it and laughed.

"Afraid?" she asked.

He simply stared at her, his chest heaving, his eyes bulging, his imagination working overtime.

She took the candle and held it over his chest.

"Trust me," she said, mockingly.

She tipped the candle. Hot wax streamed onto his chest, just below his left nipple. He flinched. Rebecca drizzled some champagne onto the wax, cooling it. Then she leaned over and licked hungrily at the foam, her tongue flicking his nipples.

She repeated the action, a bit lower this time. And she waited longer before using the champagne. He felt the hot wax sear his skin, and then the cooling champagne splashed over him, some of it trickling over his sides. Again, her mouth chased the bubbles, and when the champagne was gone, she bit his skin, but not enough to draw blood.

He could predict what was next, but was helpless to prevent it. He wasn't sure he wanted to prevent it, such was his anticipation and excitement.

From the first time he'd laid eyes on her, he'd been intensely curious. He realized that now. But here, like this, caught in a witch's brew of animal magnetism and exquisite longing, all tightly wrapped in a disintegrating cloak of innate conservative prudence, he felt tortured by conflict. He wasn't sure what he was feeling, pain or pleasure, but he knew he wanted her more than anything else in life.

She continued dripping hot wax on his body, following it with splashes of champagne, her tongue busily licking his chest, his stomach, then his navel.

She took his penis in her hand and raised the candle.

"Stop it!" he cried.

"No," she said harshly, her face a mask of sudden fury. He jerked his body in a futile attempt to escape. There was no escape. His entire body tensed as he prepared for the worst. He closed his eyes. He couldn't stand to watch.

Or not watch.

His eyes opened wide. He saw her grin, then blow out the candle, then lower her mouth around him.

The tension left, taking with it the fear. His senses were fully activated, allowing him to feel pleasure unlike any he'd known—unlike anything he'd even dreamed about.

She was incredible. A pure sex machine. Capable of giving a man supreme satisfaction.

She was also supremely dangerous.

He knew that now. But he didn't care.

She toyed with him, standing up and parading around the bed, then lying next to him and slowly stroking him. Then she would take him in her mouth and tease him with her tongue.

"Do you like it?" she needled, her eyes aglow with passion.

"I want you," he croaked.

"You want me?"

"Yes."

"I'm here."

"That's not what I mean."

"What do you mean?" she asked.

"I want to be inside you," he said.

"You want to be inside me?"

"Yes."

She kissed him on the lips. "Soon," she said. "But first, Rebecca wants to play some more."

The alarm clock woke him. For a moment he wasn't sure where he was, but then he heard Sharon groan. He reached over her to shut off the alarm as Sharon buried her head under her pillow. When Frank lay back on his own pillow, he felt a twinge of guilt.

Sharon. Jesus. What had he done?

In the calm light of morning, his rationality returned with a vengeance. As he stared at the ceiling he felt awful, realizing he'd jeopardized his marriage, even compromised his practice by having sex with Rebecca.

But as the memories of the savage night returned, he felt himself getting hard again.

It was incredible. He'd never experienced such extraordinary lust, such pure animal desire. Never before had he behaved with such total abandon, nor had he ever felt the emotions that Rebecca had succeeded in drawing from him.

He got up and padded into Michael's room, opening the wooden shutters to let in the light. He peeled back the covers. The kid was dead to the world.

Again, the guilt stabbed at him. He loved his son, his wife—his life. Sure, he and Sharon were in somewhat of a rut, but there was comfort in that, for the familiar acted like a cloak of protection.

Last night, he'd risked it all.

He rubbed his son's hair affectionately, then dropped some clothes on top of him. Michael began to stir.

"Fifteen minutes," Frank said.

His eyes still closed, Michael made a sound to indicate he was awake.

Suddenly Frank leaned over his son and kissed him on the forehead. Then he returned to the master bedroom, took off his pajamas, and stepped in the shower. The water stung as it hit his skin, and for a moment he thought he'd allowed it to get too hot. But when he lowered the temperature, the water still brought pain.

Again, the memories returned. Rebecca, her eyes bright and wide, her mouth open, her tongue flicking across her lips, her body covered in perspiration, her entire being stimulated beyond comprehension as she indulged in the very essence of her existence, the sex act, an act performed with Rebecca in full control of each and every movement.

She had enormous power, a frightening power, and Frank had fallen victim to it.

And he'd liked it.

He turned off the water, then used his towel to wipe the condensation from the mirror. It was then that he saw the source of the stinging pain. His jaw dropped. His chest and abdomen were covered in red patches, inflammations caused by the hot wax, some of them as big as pancakes.

The sight of them shamed him, and he lowered his head, leaning against the counter.

This wasn't what he wanted. Not really. He'd succumbed to curiosity and sexual desire, but now that the evidence was clearly visible, his mortification knew no bounds. The shame threatened to bring tears to his eyes.

With effort, he gathered himself together, toweled off, shaved, and brushed his teeth. He started to leave the bathroom. As he rounded the corner he almost bumped into Sharon. Quickly he covered his chest with the towel, pretending to wipe himself dry.

"Oops!" she said, then moved into the bathroom.

Had she seen the red blotches? he wondered.

Damn.

He went into the bedroom and dressed quickly.

Back in court, the presence of Rebecca turned Frank's brain into mush. She wore a white silk dress that, while neck-high, still left little to the imagination. The fluid fabric molded her curves. Her eyes smoldered with dark passion as she smiled at Frank, her lips parted, her teeth gleaming, her tongue peeking out. God! She was teasing him in front of everyone.

As they sat side by side at the defense table, waiting for the judge to arrive, she leaned toward him, placed her hand on his arm, and whispered in his ear. "You were wonderful last night."

He caught the subtle scent of her perfume.

He couldn't answer, nor could he bear to look at her. The guilt was still there, but so was her power. Conflict raged inside him, making it difficult to concentrate on the matter at hand—the trial.

He felt her hand slip away from his arm, and as it did, his nerves started screaming.

When the judge finally entered the courtroom, Frank felt a surge of relief. This was *his* element. Perhaps the pressure of his awesome responsibility would help clear his mind.

"The people would like to recall Dr. Alan Paley to the stand," Garrett announced at the beginning of another day in court.

Garrett was looking triumphant, like he had something special up his sleeve, but it was lost on Frank. Frank was shuffling papers aimlessly, still trying to pull himself together.

She was inches away from him, the aroma of her perfume bringing back memories of that reckless night of pleasure and pain. The images simply refused to leave, and for the first time in his experience, the once familiar and welcome fear in the pit of his stomach threatened to develop into full-blown panic. That would spell disaster. He had to fight it.

Garrett looked splendid in an Armani

suit, a light gray pinstripe that drew admiring glances from the women in the room. His black shoes gleamed brightly, and the power tie had been replaced by a pale yellow one. But the embroidered Stars and Stripes remained.

Judge Burnham reminded the witness he was still under oath. "And you should take it seriously," she added ominously.

Paley nodded, then, looking as nervous as before, he faced Garrett.

"Do you know Rebecca Carlson?" Garrett asked, his voice authoritative and confident.

Paley looked at Rebecca involuntarily, then jerked his head away. "Yes."

"Did you, in fact, date Miss Carlson?"

The gallery immediately started buzzing. There was so much noise, no one heard Paley's answer.

Judge Burnham smacked her gavel sharply, glared down from the bench, and shouted, "Keep your mouths shut or get out of my courtroom! This is the only time I'm going to ask nicely!"

She waited a moment for things to quiet down, then turned to the witness. "I missed your answer, Doctor."

Paley said, "Yes, we dated."

Garrett stood in front of the witness, his

arms crossed over his chest, that cocky look back on his face. Frank struggled to focus his concentration on the words.

"Did you ever discuss your patient, Mr. Marsh, with her?" Garrett asked.

"His picture was on the social page, and I mentioned that I'd treated him, yes."

"What was her reaction?"

Paley refrained from looking at Rebecca, his head rigid. "She was fascinated."

Garrett's eyebrows arched. "Did she ask you anything in particular about him?"

"She wanted to know whether cocaine would kill him if he tried it again."

"And what did you say?"

"I told her it would be Russian roulette."

Garrett turned, threw a smug smile at Frank, then said, "Your witness."

Frank stood up and moved away from the defense table. It was blessed relief. He stood ten feet away from Paley and stared at him. "Dr. Paley," he asked softly, "why didn't you mention your relationship with Rebecca earlier?"

"Nobody asked me."

Some people in the gallery tittered, but the judge's sharp stare quieted them down quickly.

Frank waited, then, continuing to speak softly, said, "Did you have sexual relations with her?"

Garrett objected immediately. "Irrelevant," he explained, almost pleading.

Frank gave the judge his best hound dog expression. "If Your Honor will allow me some latitude here, I can establish the relevance."

"You'd better," she said. "Objection overruled. The witness is directed to answer the question."

"No," Paley said.

Frank bored in, his voice gaining in power as his mental processes finally began to function. "No. That is your answer. You did *not* have sexual relations."

"No, we didn't."

"Because she refused to have sex with you, is that correct?"

Garrett could see where this was headed and moved to put a stop to it. "Objection," he cried. "Your Honor, counsel is trying to manufacture the implication that—"

The judge was beckoning again, those long red nails glowing like neon. "Get up here, both of you, right now."

The two lawyers approached the highly polished walnut bench and looked up at the judge. She was leaning on crossed arms and peering down at them, like a queen on a throne.

"Mr. Dulaney," she cautioned, "if you're

just bottom-feeding, you're going to choke on the mud."

"I'm working toward a specific point, Your Honor."

"Work fast," she told him. "I'm getting tired of seeing you this close to me."

The words were harsh, but Frank knew they were said for effect alone. Mabel was a bit of a ham, and the experienced trial lawyers knew it. When she was serious, there was a glint in her eye that shone like a torch. When a lawyer saw the glint, he was well advised to tread carefully. But here, now, there was no glint.

"Yes, Your Honor," Frank said, his tone reverent.

"Objection overruled," she announced to those in the room.

Frank and Garrett returned to their positions. Frank worked hard to suppress a smile. Rebecca had provided him with evidence that would take care of Dr. Paley, and as he stole a glance at her now, he saw her smiling, that adoring look in her eyes.

He turned and faced the witness. "Do you remember your last date with Rebecca, at the Cat and Fiddle Restaurant?"

Paley's nervousness went up three notches. His face blanched, and he squirmed uncomfortably in his seat. "It wasn't that memorable," he said.

"Well, do you remember trying to force yourself on her in the parking lot?"

Garrett was on his feet, his arm in the air, his eyes blazing. But Frank overrode his objection by saying, "Because I can bring in the parking-lot attendant and two customers to freshen up your memory if I need to!"

He thought he detected a smirk on Judge Burnham's lips as she looked at Garrett and said, "I didn't hear the reason for your objection, Mr. Garrett."

Garrett, red-faced, rubbed his forehead for a moment, then shook his head and sat down.

"Wasn't that the last time you saw her until you appeared in court, Dr. Paley?" Frank asked.

Paley, clearly embarrassed, now turned sullen. "I told you I don't remember the last time I saw her."

It was always a mistake for a witness to argue with an experienced trial lawyer, but most of the belligerent ones didn't seem to understand how really stupid it was. Paley was about to find out.

"In fact," Frank said, "didn't you attempt to blackmail Rebecca into seeing you again by threatening to testify falsely against her?"

Paley gripped the railing tightly as he shouted, "No! You're crazy!"

It was exactly the answer Frank was hoping for. He turned away from the witness and walked to the defense table. First he looked at a smiling Rebecca, then at a grinning Gabe, who also knew what was coming.

Frank removed a tape recorder from his briefcase and held it aloft. "Your Honor," he said, "I have a tape from Rebecca's answering machine which I'd like to play now."

Garrett was incensed. "Objection. Your Honor, we don't know where this tape is from or who made it or under what circumstances."

Frank was halfway to the bench, a folder in his hands. "Your Honor, I have reports from two independent audio labs that Mr. Garrett has himself used to verify evidence in other trials. Both of them concluded that the voice on the tape was recorded over the telephone and that there's been no tampering."

He handed the folder to Judge Burnham. She scanned the documents for a moment, then mumbled, "Hoisted on your own petard, Mr. Garrett."

Frank smiled inwardly. They were exactly the words he would have used.

Her reading over, the judge said, "I'll allow it."

Frank could see Garrett was outraged, but there was nothing the prosecutor could do. It was folly to argue with a judge once a ruling had been made. The prosecutor could do nothing but fulminate silently.

Frank walked back to the table, placed the tape recorder on it, then depressed the play button. A beep preceded Paley's voice, which boomed across the hushed courtroom. It was immediately obvious the man was drunk.

"Rebecca . . . I know you're there. Goddammit. Pick up the phone. You think I won't do it?"

There was the sound of a phone being slammed down, then another beep. Then Paley's voice again.

"You'll be screwing *women* for life, Rebecca. I can put you away. You'd better call me or you're fucked . . ." A mean, cruel laugh. "Either one way or the other."

Again, the sound of the phone being slammed down violently.

Frank waited for the room to absorb the words. The only sound was a muffled cough toward the back of the room.

"What did you mean, Dr. Paley?" he asked the badly shaken witness.

Paley simply shook his head, speechless.

Frank turned and faced the jury as he asked the next question. "You never told her about Andrew Marsh, did you?"

Paley found his voice. "Yes, I did!" he exclaimed. "She asked me, and I told her."

Frank whirled and stared at him. "Perjury is a criminal charge, Doctor!"

"I'm not lying."

Frank looked at the jury, his face expressing his complete disgust. He waited for effect, then said, "No further questions."


Court was adjourned for the day. The army of reporters crowded around Rebecca as she, Frank, and Gabe tried to make their way to the elevator, Frank and Gabe flanking the blond woman, trying to protect her from the bulk of people. Frank carried his jacket over his shoulder, feeling good, confident.

"You were brilliant," Rebecca said, clutching his arm.

"I didn't break him all the way."

Gabe would have none of it. "You burned him *down*," he exulted.

They shuffled into a crowded elevator.

In the massive press of bodies, Gabe was separated from Rebecca and Frank, who huddled in the corner next to each other.

"Press P-1 for me, Gabe," Frank said, standing on his toes to talk over the heads of the others.

Gabe pressed P-1 and P-2.

Her movements concealed from the crowd, Rebecca rested her hand on Frank's butt, then grinned up at him innocently. Then he felt her fingers snake between his legs. Embarrassed, he lifted his briefcase to push her arm away. But the moment he relaxed, he realized what her other hand was doing.

Hidden by the briefcase, her hand was slowly opening his fly.

He looked down at her and grimaced, shaking his head, but her attention was elsewhere, her head pointed toward the front of the elevator, a bored expression already fixed on her face in case someone turned around.

He was seized by a sense of panic. He couldn't say anything, for it would draw attention to what this wild woman was doing. He cleared his throat in an effort to get her attention. Rebecca smiled, but refused to look at him, all the while continuing to work the zipper.

The elevator reached P-1 and the door opened. Gabe stepped off along with some other people and called over his shoulder, "See you tomorrow."

Frank could not speak. Rebecca's hand was now inside his trousers, fondling him in an elevator with people just inches away. If one happened to turn their head and look down—

Jesus. He was getting an erection. Impossible. If anything, it should have shriveled up and tried to hide. But no. It was growing, no longer a part of him. Now it belonged to her, and followed her demands.

"P-4, please," Rebecca said, straight-faced.

Someone pressed P-4. Rebecca kept at it, working her hand inside the fly of his shorts, her hand now wrapped around his penis, stroking it to almost painful full erection.

Frank was sweating now, red-faced, mortified, unable to move or speak. At each floor, people got off the elevator. By the time it reached P-3, Frank and Rebecca were alone. Rebecca had his penis out of his pants, completely exposed, her hand working busily. The doors of the elevator closed.

He was angry. He wanted to stop this

craziness. But it was also exhilarating, exciting, wild, uninhibited, and most of all, dangerous. Perhaps it was the combination of passion and danger that stopped him from screaming at her.

She wrapped a leg around him, placed both hands on his butt, and began rubbing herself against him.

The elevator door opened to the last level of the parking garage, smelling of car exhaust and oil and mildew. She was draped all over him, her breasts hard against his chest. He could feel their heat through his thin shirt.

"Someone's going to see us," he said as he tried to look around.

Without a word, she pulled away from him and walked away.

He thought it was over, but it wasn't. Fascinated, he watched as Rebecca climbed onto the hood of a car. She removed a shoe and, shielding her eyes with one arm, swung the shoe at a light fixture hanging from the low concrete ceiling. The light shattered into a hundred shards of glass, the shards spraying everywhere, including the hood of the car.

It was dim now, Rebecca barely visible in the shadows. He walked toward her. She was sitting on the hood of the car, and as he approached she leaned back on her elbows, oblivious to the broken pieces of glass around her, and spread her legs.

She didn't care.

She wanted him. Here. Now. It was obvious. He could see it in her eyes, now that he was inches away from her.

"I want you inside me," she said huskily.

For a moment he thought he was having a nightmare, a hallucination of some kind, a crazy flashback. This was insanity! But looking at her, hearing her heavy breathing, smelling her perfume, all thoughts of propriety fled, and when she placed her hand between his legs and pulled him closer, he was consumed with but one thought. The rest of the world disappeared from view, out of sight and out of his conscious mind.

It was as if he was mindless, an automaton programmed to provide whatever Rebecca wanted upon demand. He was helpless, a slave to his need.

He pulled her panties down, bending one knee through the leg hole, leaving them hooked around one ankle. Then he pulled her skirt up out of the way and worked himself inside her.

She leaned back, and as she did he heard the terrible sound of glass crunching.

Jesus! The glass was cutting her. He pulled away. She grabbed at him and pulled him back.

"Don't stop. Don't worry," she said throatily.

Her eyes were wide, covered with a thin film of moisture. Her mouth was open and her tongue flicked along her lower lip.

For a brief instant his intellect almost brought him to his senses, but only for an instant. Once again, he was lost, drowning in a sea of lust, surrendering to madness, completely out of control, raw animal concupiscence pushing all rational thought aside.

He thrust himself inside her and felt her hot wetness engulf him. His heart was pounding again, his hands trembling with excitement. He felt her hands on his face, hands that seemed to burn his skin just as the hot wax had the previous night.

Suddenly Rebecca rolled out from under him and forced him back against the hood of the car. He felt the sudden pain of the glass as it cut through his shirt and pierced his flesh. He bit his tongue and muffled a scream, and it sounded more like a hiss.

He couldn't stop. He kept thrusting, kneading her breasts through her dress, bending up to kiss her face, driven by forces he no longer controlled.

Rebecca's eyes widened with excitement when she saw the blood seeping through his expensive cotton shirt. It seemed to spur her on, and she picked up the rhythm, her hips first grinding, then moving back and forth violently, the sound of their bodies slamming together echoing throughout the concrete-walled garage.

It didn't matter. Nothing mattered. Just sex.

Frank was screwing a woman—or being screwed, he wasn't sure which—on the shattered-glass-covered hood of someone's car while it was parked in a public garage. Not just a woman, but his client. Pieces of glass were stuck in his back, and the blood was spreading all over his shirt. If he was found in this situation, his career would probably be over. So would his marriage.

His whole life would be down the drain.

But he didn't care.

All he cared about was being inside her.

A deep moan escaped his lips as Rebecca brought him to the edge. Her breath was hot on his cheek, beads of sweat popping out on her forehead. Her eyes were glazed as she continued to pick up the pace.

And then he exploded with a violent

shudder, an orgasm so strong he thought his heart would burst.

There, on the hood of a car parked in the garage of the courthouse where he made his living.

And he didn't care.

◆It was Michael's night at karate school, and Frank was to pick him up. That was the routine. Sharon would drop Michael off on her way to the restaurant and Frank was to pick him up and bring him home.

Frank, his mind still spinning from the turbulent excitement of less than an hour ago, parked the car and walked toward the entrance of the school.

The cool, damp air stung his cheeks. His legs felt rubbery. His hands trembled. He felt disoriented and confused.

His life was upside down, distorted, terribly out of kilter. Everything he'd ever understood was now a mystery, for nothing made sense. He could feel the ground beneath him and see the sky above, but he didn't trust his senses anymore. Maybe the sky was below and the ground above.

He felt as if he were no longer human, but some fanciful Dali creation, a twisted figure trapped within a surrealistic painting. He was on display in Rebecca's gallery with lights shining on him.

Rebecca was there with people, all of them leaning forward and staring at the painting, then touching it. Touching Frank. Rebecca was laughing and explaining how this was her prize possession.

He shook his head to rid himself of the frightening images. He was only partly successful.

He saw his son standing and talking outside the karate school, dressed like the others, their white pajamalike uniforms almost glowing in the dark.

Michael saw him approach and loped happily away from his friends. As he neared his father he spun around, positioned his arms and hands, and did some kicks. Then he danced around his father, making more karate moves, accompanying them with a series of guttural grunts and shrieking yells. He was fired up.

Finally he backed up and playfully butted Frank in the back with his head. Frank howled in pain.

"That wasn't hard!" Michael exclaimed.

The pain was excruciating, slivers of it

transecting the length and breadth of his back. Frank valiantly fought it off, wiping the tears from his eyes. Michael looked puzzled.

"You're getting too good," Frank explained, putting an arm around his son and walking him to the car. He wanted no more accidental contact with his back.

The trip home took them by the docks and past Rebecca's houseboat. As they approached the bridge Frank could see it, its nearness drawing his attention like a magnet. Soft light glowed behind the drawn curtains.

Michael had been keeping up a steady patter since they'd left the karate school, but Frank now tuned him out. He wondered what Rebecca was doing at this moment. Just the thought of her intensified his pain. His back throbbed. His left knee started to quiver.

Was she alone? Was she thinking of him?

He'd always considered her dangerous, but this . . . this was beyond dangerous.

"I got my foot up high," Michael was saying. "Joey didn't see it coming. I'd left myself open, but I was fast. You gotta be fast. The teacher bowed to me!"

He let out a yell that made Frank jump.

"Do you know what that means?" Michael asked.

Frank hadn't heard a word. "No," he said. "What?"

"It's the highest compliment you can get."

Frank's eyes were still fixed on the houseboat. Finally it disappeared behind him. He almost sighed with relief.

"And you know what I did?" Michael continued, "I bowed right back to him."

"Who?" Frank asked.

There was a hesitation, and then he heard his son say, "You weren't listening." Michael's little-boy voice was accusatory.

"Sure I was," Frank protested. "You kicked Joey."

Michael sighed. "Who cares? The teacher bowed to me."

"That's great," he said.

He must have missed something, he thought, because Michael stopped talking and stared sullenly out the window.

"That's terrific," Frank said, trying to get through.

Nothing.

The hell with it. He had his own problems.

◆ ◆ ◆

When they arrived home, Frank stripped, took a shower, then put some salve on his wounds. At least the bleeding had stopped, but the wounds were ugly looking. Over a dozen, some of them as long as half an inch. He bent himself like a pretzel, standing in front of the mirror, trying to see if there were any bits of glass still stuck in his skin. It didn't appear so. He ran his hand over his skin, but felt no glass.

He changed into fresh clothes, then grabbed the bloodstained shirt, rolled it up into a ball, and took it to the trash bin in the kitchen. There, he shoved it down to the bottom, under some containers from Sharon's restaurant. Not good enough. He lifted out the plastic container and tied it shut, then carried it out back and put it in a garbage pail.

Back in the kitchen, he poured himself a beer. As he sat alone at the table he noticed his right hand was shaking. And why not? Every encounter with Rebecca resulted in physical damage being inflicted. First it was the wax, and now the glass. Jesus. If this escalated, what would be next?

He shuddered. She was like a narcotic. He wanted more, and the hell with the danger. The realization of that fact frightened him. He'd always been in control of his life, known exactly what he wanted and gone after it. Even as a kid, he'd known. When he was old enough to comprehend that a pro hockey career was out of the question, he set his sights on being a lawyer.

And when he fell in love with Sharon, he found a way to have her and still pursue the dream. He'd made it, too. Because he knew what he wanted and went after it.

Now nothing made sense. His world was upside down, all because of his inability to resist the sexual charms of a woman who might well be out of her mind. The worst possible kind of relationship. Stupid, stupid.

But just thinking of her made him hard again.

He groaned. Michael was in the front room watching television. Throughout dinner, Michael had said nothing, barely picking at his food. Frank realized he'd wounded his son with his insensitivity, but nothing he'd said changed anything.

Now he wanted to try again.

He walked to the front room and sat beside his son.

"Michael?"

His son ignored him.

Frank grabbed his arm. Michael winced.

"Look," Frank said, "someday you'll be all grown up and facing the same kind of problems I face every day. I'm sorry I was off somewhere in outer space. I really am."

"It's okay."

"It's not okay," Frank said. "But it's important to me that you understand the reasons. Why don't I shut off the television, and we'll talk. Just for a while. Okay?"

Michael made a face. Frank grabbed the remote and shut off the TV.

"Can you look at me?" he asked.

Michael looked at him, a pout on his lips.

"I'm a lawyer," Frank began.

"I know that."

"Okay. You know what's going on?"

"I think so. You got this trial. The woman who killed that old guy."

Frank almost bit his tongue. "Did it ever occur to you that she's innocent?"

"If you say so, Dad."

"Not because I say so, but because she really is innocent."

"Then how come they arrested her?"

"Because that happens sometimes. Not often, but more often than most people think. In Rebecca Carlson's case, there are people who don't like her very much. They're saying things that make it appear she's guilty, but she isn't."

"Okay."

"Okay. Now put yourself in my shoes. I'm her lawyer. That means I'm the only person standing between her and a long jail term. If I make a mistake, she could be found guilty. On the other hand, if I do my job as well as I'm capable, there's a strong chance she'll be set free.

"So, in fact, her life is in my hands. That's a fearsome responsibility. It can be terrifying at times. And there are times when thinking about it makes me a little crazy. Like tonight."

"Is that what you were thinking about?"

"Yes. I'm worried, Michael. If I screw up, this woman is going to go to jail, probably for twenty years. That's a long time to spend in jail for something you didn't do. So, I was thinking about the trial, thinking about what went on today, and thinking about what I have to do tomorrow.

"But just because I'm preoccupied doesn't mean I don't love you or care about you. I love you very much. You and your mother are the most important people in the world, and always will be.

"But there are times when I don't act like it."

Michael smiled. Frank smiled back at him.

"You understand?" he asked.

"Sure, Dad."

He gave Michael a hug, and Michael hugged him back. The pressure on his back made the pain excruciating.

He pulled away and said, "Now, tell me again about this bowing stuff, okay."

With Michael tucked away in bed, Frank watched the eleven o'clock news. The trial was the lead item. There was a clip of Rebecca and Frank as they left the courtroom, and as the camera zoomed in on Rebecca's face, Frank's back started throbbing again.

And his hands started trembling.

He switched off the TV, moved to the bedroom, threw on a T-shirt, and crawled into bed, exhausted and confused. For a while he stared at the darkness, his mind a whirl of bizarre thoughts. Then, finally, he drifted off to sleep.

He was still asleep when Sharon came home and crawled into bed beside him.

She was still charged from the excitement of another night at the café. It always took her about a half-hour to come down to earth.

Frank's back was to her, and as she pulled the covers back his soft buns glowed in the reflected light of the bedside lamp.

She reached out and ran her hand over the soft skin, caressing it gently. Then she started to lift his T-shirt gingerly. The motion disturbed him and he rolled over on his back, let out a grunt, then rolled on his side.

Now he was facing her, still asleep.

She sighed, wound her legs around his, then closed her eyes.

The sunshine almost blinded him as he drove to court. It was a glorious day, cool and dry, but Frank's emotions were still a boiling caldron of confusion. The face of Rebecca seemed to float in front of his eyes, her eyes beckoning him, her full lips parted, her tongue licking her lips.

He drove into the parking garage. The contrast in light was so great, he had to stop until his eyes fully adjusted. Then he continued to the parking spot assigned to attorneys.

He met Rebecca at her car. As usual, she looked radiant, her hair carefully arranged, her eyes as sultry as ever.

"Good morning," she said cheerfully.

"Hi."

She grabbed his hand. He pulled it away.

"What's the matter?" she asked.

"Nothing," he said. "I just want to concentrate on what's ahead."

She turned and walked toward the elevator. He followed.

Neither spoke.

As they walked down the corridor the reporters clustered around, as usual. And, as usual, Frank had nothing to say. Someone pushed him in the back and he almost cried out. But he didn't. He kept moving, through the doors, and back into a packed courtroom.

There was an electricity in the room, a sense of anticipation. Yesterday's testimony had been dramatic, and on the morning news broadcast, an embarrassed Robert Garrett had promised some fireworks.

Just words, Frank had thought as he watched his adversary on television.

But they were more than words. The explosion came after the afternoon recess.

After a series of uninteresting witnesses, some of the spectators had actually fallen asleep. Garrett was waiting for a special moment. Now he stood up, slowly buttoned his jacket, and asked the court to call Jeffrey Roston to the stand.

Frank, suddenly alert, looked at Rebecca. The name meant nothing to him. It wasn't on the witness list, and no deposition had been taken.

When he saw the shocked expression on his client's face, it was clear that Roston's name rang a bell with Rebecca. She was as tight as a violin string, her face pale, her mouth open, her chest heaving as she took short, shallow breaths.

"Do you know him?" Frank whispered urgently.

Rebecca didn't answer. She was looking over her shoulder at a man entering the room, a handsome man in his fifties, with graying hair and a steady walk.

Frank whirled and faced the judge. "Permission to approach?"

Judge Burnham beckoned.

Garrett joined him at the bench.

"Your Honor," Frank said, "this witness has never been mentioned by the prosecution and is not on the witness list. I ask that this testimony be delayed until such time as we've had the chance to depose the witness."

The judge looked at Garrett, a bored expression on her face. It had not been an exciting day to this point.

"Our investigators didn't contact Mr. Roston until yesterday afternoon in New York," Garrett explained. "He's an ex-lover of the defendant's."

"What took so long?" Judge Burnham asked.

"He just came home from an extended vacation."

"No matter," Frank insisted. "We are entitled to depose the witness, Your Honor."

She thought for a moment, then said, "All right. I'm going to allow the testimony. If you need some time to prepare for proper cross-examination, I'll allow it, but I want this trial kept moving."

Frank was livid. "Your Honor—"

A glance stopped him. "That's it, counselor. Take a seat."

As he returned to the defense table the look on Rebecca's face troubled Frank. She was still in shock and it showed. He had constantly warned her not to react to anything that took place in the courtroom lest the jurors misinterpret her expressions. It was always better to project an inscrutable expression.

Until now she'd been excellent, but here, at this moment, she looked terrified. She'd either forgotten or was ignoring his advice, and he gave her a look as he sat down. It changed nothing.

Damn.

Garrett positioned himself so that the spectators and jurors could see the witness unhindered. Garrett seemed full of himself, confident again, relishing what lay ahead. The tone of his voice reflected that renewed confidence.

"Mr. Roston," he began, "what was your relationship with Miss Carlson?"

"We were lovers," the man answered calmly.

"How long were you together?" Garrett asked.

"For about a year."

"How would you describe your sex life with her?"

Roston squirmed a little. "It was . . . very intense."

Frank clearly understood that answer. He felt his own body tensing. Intense. Good word for it. He shifted in his chair.

"I know this is very personal," Garrett said softly, "but I'm going to ask you to be more specific."

Roston looked ruffled. "She was always trying to get me more and more worked up."

"By what means?"

"I couldn't *do* everything she wanted in my condition."

"What condition is that?"

"I had a bad heart," Roston said.

There was a collective gasp from the spectators. Despite his years of experience, Frank's own jaw dropped open. Garrett looked at him and smiled, obviously pleased that Frank was so shocked. The prosecutor waited before continuing.

Frank could feel Rebecca's hand touching his. Angry, he pulled away. Something else he would normally never do with a client.

"What happened next?" Garrett asked.

"I had bypass surgery."

"And how are you now?"

"Fine. The doctors say I can live to be a very old man."

"How did your relationship with the defendant progress after you had the surgery?"

There was bitterness in the answer. "It ground to a sudden halt. She left me."

Frank stared straight ahead, trying to keep his face impassive. Out of the corner of his eye, he could see Rebecca staring at him, looking perplexed and hurt. The shock was gone. Now she presented an image of a woman in pain, betrayed somehow, though Frank couldn't imagine why. He turned his attention back to Garrett's direct examination.

"When did she say she was leaving?" Garrett asked.

"She didn't. She just left."

"Why do you think she left you?"

"I think she realized I wasn't going to die."

Frank, mesmerized by what was happening, objected after the question was answered, a rookie move. "Objection," he cried. "The question calls for a conclusion on the part of the witness."

Judge Burnham looked at Frank. She could see he was distracted, almost discombobulated. She felt sympathy. "The question's been answered, counsel. Are you moving to strike?"

Frank felt like an idiot. In a soft voice he said, "Motion to strike."

Garrett wasn't about to lose his advantage. "Your Honor, the witness dated Miss Carlson for many months. His opinion is a valid means of substantiating her character."

Frank, with great effort, finally snapped partly out of his funk. He was on his feet, gesticulating, some power back in his voice. "The opinion of a rejected lover is biased," he said.

The judge took little time. "Motion granted."

Garrett continued with his line of questioning. "Did Miss Carlson ever give you any indication why she was leaving?"

Frank's faculties were still not at full song, but his instincts were there. "Objection," he said. "The witness has already stated that she left without an explanation."

The judge nodded, then turned to Garrett. "Mr. Garrett, I suggest you move along to another line of questioning."

Garrett took a deep breath, then asked, "When you say your sexual relations with Miss Carlson were intense, in what way?"

Roston squirmed in the chair. "It was as if she were trying to push me as far as she could."

"Can you give the court an example?"

Roston nodded. "Sex was a game with her. She got off on the control. She always used to tell me it had to be her way."

Frank could hear Rebecca stirring uncomfortably beside him. She was squirming in her seat, the toe of her shoe tapping the floor nervously. He looked at her, but she was staring at Roston, her eyes filled with anger, her lips pursed tightly, her hands balled into fists.

Frank looked at the jurors. Two of them

were staring at Rebecca, the expressions on their faces clear evidence of what they were thinking.

Frank felt the air leave his lungs. He wanted to sink through the floor. Roston's words were true, he knew. Roston had lived it and Frank had lived it. And how many others? Always the same. Rebecca in control.

Now he was reliving it again. Jesus. He could hardly think.

He heard Roston say, "A few nights before the bypass, I woke up . . . she'd tied me to the bed with my own belt."

The crowd behind Frank snickered.

Judge Burnham banged her gavel. To Frank, it was the sound of someone hammering a railway spike into his skull.

The crowd quiet, Garrett asked, "What did she say after she tied you up with your own belt?"

Roston was becoming extremely uncomfortable. Frank could empathize. No man liked to sit in front of a crowd of strangers and recite the many ways he'd been made to look the fool.

The sound of Garrett's booming voice brought Frank back to reality. Barely.

"Mr. Roston, I know this is difficult for you," Garrett said, "but it's important. Please tell the court."

Roston exhaled some air. "She said she was going to fuck me like I'd never been fucked before."

The gallery was pure pandemonium. People were laughing and shouting and slapping their knees in glee. Judge Burnham had had enough of it. As promised, she slammed her gavel down a few times, then said, "Bailiff, clear the courtroom except for the reporters."

There were immediate howls of protest, but the bailiff kept moving them out, shooing them like cattle being led into pens. It took a while, but the judge refused to call a recess. This was her court and *she* was in control. They would wait.

When the room was empty, save for those reporters allowed to remain, the judge ordered Garrett to continue his examination of Mr. Roston.

With most of the spectators gone, Garrett's voice echoed in the high-ceilinged room. "After she tied you up, Mr. Roston, what did she do next?"

Roston seemed in agony. "She started . . . masturbating . . . and telling me how much she wanted me inside her. It drove me crazy."

Garrett couldn't help it. He took a long look at Rebecca. So did everyone else in the room. Rebecca was staring straight ahead, her face a mask of indifference, the anger gone. She looked guilty as hell.

Garrett, full of confidence, turned back to Roston. "Hadn't your doctor told you to avoid exertion?"

Roston sighed. "You don't think about it at right that moment. You don't think at all."

Frank cringed involuntarily. He wished he were somewhere else. Anyplace else. The words of this witness were hitting him hard. He felt sick. Weak. He felt short of breath.

"Did your heart start to bother you?" Garrett asked.

Roston slowly nodded. "We started to make love . . . she was on top of me . . . and every time I got close . . . ."

"To orgasm?"

"Yes. She'd stop. I couldn't take it. My heart was pounding so hard I thought my eardrums were going to break. I couldn't breathe . . . I was suffocating . . . I begged her . . . I really thought I was about to die."

Garrett took a step forward. "What did she say when you begged her?"

Roston's face filled with hate. "She laughed."

Garrett took a moment, then asked,

"Did you change your will while you were involved with Miss Carlson?"

"Yes."

"Who was your primary beneficiary?"

"She was." He uttered a sour laugh. "I'm a fool."

*Fool.* The word struck Frank like a hammer blow.

Garrett wound it up. "Thank you, Mr. Roston. No further questions."

Frank wanted to stand up, but he knew his legs would betray him. He also knew he couldn't bear to ask questions of this witness. It would be like cross-examining himself. He couldn't do that. Not now, at least. He needed to pull himself together.

"No questions at this time," he said softly, "but I would like to cross-examine the witness after I've had the opportunity to study the testimony."

Beside him, Rebecca lowered her head, as if trying to hide from the stares of everyone in the room.

Judge Burnham looked at the wall clock, then said, "That's fine, Mr. Dulaney. You may cross-examine the witness tomorrow. It's after four o'clock. The court will adjourn until tomorrow morning."

She stood up and swept toward her chambers, her black robe trailing behind her like a huge kite. The reporters hurried out of the room, ready to hit the pay phones or climb into their electronic-equipment-filled trucks.

Garrett tidied up, put some folders in his briefcase, then smiled at Frank. "You're dead in the water," he said.

Frank, his legs still rubbery, walked past him without a word. Garrett held the wooden gate for Rebecca. Her hips grazed him as she passed through.

Then she looked at him and said, "You're enjoying the testimony, aren't you, Bob?"

"Beats a holdup at some 7-Eleven," he quipped.

She laughed. A nice laugh. Garrett liked her laugh. And she had guts. As she walked out of the courtroom her back was as straight as a drill sergeant's, her head was held high, and there was a seductive sway to her hips.

In the corridor, Rebecca hurried to catch Frank. Drawing beside him, she said, "I can explain."

There were reporters in the corridor, but he didn't care. He grabbed her wrist and shoved her into an empty courtroom, then spun her around to face him.

"You're a little *late*," he bellowed, his

voice echoing throughout the room. "I needed to know *before* he testified. Why the fuck didn't you warn me at least?"

"I didn't expect him either," she protested. "Did you need to hear about every man I ever had sex with?"

He was beside himself with rage. Just barely, he restrained himself from slapping her across the mouth. "Just the ones with bad hearts who put you in their wills!"

Her eyes widened. "You think I killed Andrew."

"So does everybody in the courtroom! You made me look like shit in there."

Now she was incensed. "*You're* not on trial."

"Oh, the hell I'm not. I was out of my *mind* to get involved with you."

"To make love to me?"

"Yes! But I don't want to *compound* my mistakes. You're my client, that's it. I don't want to have anything to do with you beyond that."

It was amazing. Her moods were mercurial. One minute she was raging like a tigress, the next displaying deep hurt. The look on her face now was so sincere, so real—

"Just like that?" she asked. "Like I don't

have any feelings? Like I don't matter?"

"Hey," he said bitterly, "I'm not your type. I'm too young and healthy."

Tears formed at the corners of her eyes. "That's not fair."

"No," he said coldly, "but it's accurate."

She stared at him for a moment, the picture of wounded pride. But then her face hardened and she said, "Fuck you, too, Frank."

Then she turned on her heel and stormed out of the courtroom.

As always, the coffeehouse was jam-packed. The usual uptown crowd milled about the entrance while they waited for a seat at the bar or a table.

Frank walked past them all, through the door, and into the room. He smelled the coffee and the food, but this time they almost turned his stomach. He felt the hot stares of some who recognized him, but he kept his head down and bullied his way through. The babble of voices hurt his ears.

He saw Garrett sitting at a table, deep in conversation with another lovely woman. Jesus. The man had a veritable harem, all of them gorgeous, intelligent-looking women. The man was good-looking, charming even, but this was ridiculous. There had to be a secret to his success.

Frank wondered if Garrett had a touch of the same magic Rebecca possessed. Something supernatural and evil.

As Garrett spoke, the woman gazed into his eyes, hanging on his every word as if Garrett were some guru from India. She was totally oblivious to the envious stares she was getting from the women around her. But Frank saw them.

He tried to pass the table without being noticed.

He failed.

Garrett, as if he had eyes in the back of his head, grabbed Frank's jacket and held him fast, like a security guard grabbing a shoplifting kid in a candy store.

His haughty face was flushed with victory, his mouth formed in a smirk. He beamed, hamming it up for all to see, very aware of the stares *he* was receiving.

"First time I ever nailed you!" he crowed. "That was a sweet moment."

"Enjoy it while you can," Frank said, pulling away. Another second, he thought, and he'd be driving his fist into Garrett's insolent face.

He made it to the espresso bar, where

Sharon was drawing cups of cappuccino, two at a time. He leaned on the counter and pasted a fake smile on his lips.

"Hi," he chirped. "Where's Michael?"

She kept working, not looking at him. She looked pale and tired. Maybe the long hours were finally catching up with her.

"I took him to spend the night at Kevin's," she said softly.

That was a surprise. "Why didn't you tell me?" he said, angry at her insensitivity to his work. "I could have stayed at the office. I've got a shitload of work."

She finally looked at him, her expression one of deep hurt. She seemed about to burst into tears.

"Is something wrong?" Frank asked.

Sharon gathered herself together, leaned forward, and tried to keep her voice low, but with all the racket in the restaurant it was impossible.

"You mean you could've used the time to screw your client," she said.

A waitress stood beside Frank, wide-eyed, having heard the remark.

"That's paranoid," Frank said quickly.

"Oh, man—"

Sharon whirled away from him and walked directly into a busboy. A tray of dirty dishes hit the floor with a thunderous crash. Everyone stopped talking and stared. Then someone applauded. Probably Garrett, Frank thought.

Sharon, almost in tears, patted the busboy on the back and apologized. The buzz of conversation picked up as Sharon strode to the kitchen. Frank was right behind her.

He chased her through the kitchen, ignoring the puzzled stares of the staff. She was out the door, into the alley behind the place, walking away quickly, almost running.

The alley was used to service the stores that backed onto it. A place for trucks to deliver and pick up, dark, dirty, littered with dumpsters, garbage cans, and piles of garbage-filled plastic bags. Dim light bulbs hung over doors marked SHIPPING AND RECEIVING. A small river of dank water meandered down the middle of the alley.

"Sharon," Frank called after her.

She looked over her shoulder. "Go away!"

Wondering what the hell was wrong, he cried, "Talk to me."

She kept moving.

He grabbed her elbow. She kicked at him. His mouth fell open in utter shock. She'd never gotten physical before.

"What *is* it?" he cried, almost begging.

She told him. "People see your car down at the river, in front of her houseboat," she said, "it gets *back* to me."

So that was it. He felt his heart begin to pound.

"She's my client!" he exclaimed quickly. "I'm allowed to have conferences with my client."

"Sure you are," she countered, pointing at him accusingly. "Why don't you have them in your office?"

He threw his hands in the air. "I can't believe you'd listen to bullshit gossip."

"I talked to her," she said, her voice harsh with fury.

He was stunned. "What? When?"

Her eyes were filled with hate. "She called here tonight, looking for you."

His nerves were screaming at him. Jesus. He tried to concentrate. "What'd she tell you?"

Sharon looked at the dark sky, then at Frank. "I could hear it in her voice, how she said your name."

"You're making this up," he said.

Her eyes were like daggers, stabbing at him. "What'd she do to you, Frank? How'd you get those marks on your chest?"

He felt the blood draining from his face.

His hands began to tingle.

Her dreadful hurt had metamorphosed quickly. Rage took its place. She stood there, her hands balled into fists, her eyes full of tears that refused to spill over, her entire body rigid.

"Were they bites?" she asked. "What were they? Don't you think I know what happened to your back?"

He felt his heart stop. He could hardly breathe. He wanted to loosen his tie, but his arm wouldn't move. Again, strange images captured his brain, turning his mind into a fog of confusion and dismay.

"Jesus," he said softly.

She knew! She knew it all. His worst fears had been realized.

He'd known from the start it was dangerous. But Rebecca had been so unrelenting, so single-minded—so goddamn powerful. He'd succumbed without much of a fight, at first aware of the hazards, then throwing caution to the winds to satisfy a mysterious, never-before-felt need he couldn't understand, even now.

Rebecca had emasculated him, and now he was to pay the price.

"I had this dumb idea that we were happy!" Sharon screamed, letting it all out now that the dreaded subject had been broached. She could see the truth in his eyes. His denials were lies. *Her* worst fears had been realized, her bluff painfully called.

"I thought we were good together," she said. "We're supposed to be a family, Frank. I made a commitment to you. . . . I trusted you."

He could barely speak. There was no use denying it. She had him cold. What could he say? He struggled to find the words, but he knew instinctively that any words were useless. Just empty words. Just more bull-shit.

"It doesn't have anything to do with you," he croaked finally.

As he feared, it didn't help.

"You son of a bitch," she screamed. "How dare you stand there and tell me that?"

"I love you," he pleaded. "You're my wife."

She shook her head. "You're an egotistical, lying prick. Go pack some clothes. I don't want to see you when I get home."

He wanted to die. He felt awful. "Sharon, please . . . I don't want to lose you."

She was resolute. Bitterly, she said "Then you shouldn't have fucked her."

She walked past him, back into the coffeehouse. Frank hung his head in utter
humiliation. He never saw Garrett watching them through the back window.

He was consumed with rage. He was in
trouble, serious trouble, all because he'd
been suckered by a conniving, charismatic
bitch with a penchant for raunchy sex
games.

He was as angry at himself as he was at
Rebecca. Sure, she was a witch, but he'd
allowed her to cast her spell on him. What
did that make him?

A fool.

He kicked at the ground, then started
toward the rear door of the restaurant.

No. The hell with it. He'd walk around.
He didn't want Sharon to see him—or that
smarmy bastard Garrett either.

He took the long way around, got into
his car, and slammed the key into the ignition. Blue smoke poured from the tires of
the car as he pulled away, slid around a
corner, and headed toward the docks.

He ran red lights, went through stop
signs, even let his speed get up to seventy in
some places. He broke every traffic law in
the book. It didn't really matter. His life was
a joke. Ruined. He was in a blind rage.

He expected to see flashing red-and-blue

lights behind him any minute, but by some miracle, he didn't. And when he arrived at the houseboat, he slammed the car door shut, almost running to the door of Rebecca's place.

The door was unlocked. He charged through and took the stairs two at a time, bursting into the bedroom with fire in his eyes.

She was lying on the large bed, with its pink satin sheets and thick comforter pulled back, going over some photographs, her hair in disarray, looking very sexy in a red silk robe embroidered with yellow fire-eating dragons. It suited her.

She seemed shocked to see him.

"What the hell'd you say to my wife!" he screamed.

"Nothing," she said innocently. "I asked if you were there, and you weren't."

She got up from the bed. He grabbed her by the shoulders and shook her—hard. The robe slipped open, revealing the fact that she was naked under it. Her pink-tipped breasts taunted him. She made no effort to cover herself.

"Frank, I didn't say a damn thing," she repeated.

"Why'd you call?" he asked.

She looked hurt. In a soft voice she said,

"I wanted to know if I still had a lawyer."

He pushed her again. "You are such a liar!"

Her mood changed quickly. She placed her hands on her hips and sneered at him. "Oh," she said, mocking him, "you think I told her all the nasty details?" She waved a hand in the air. "Maybe I gave her some advice. What do you think? A couple of pointers?"

"Goddamnit!" he screamed. Then he pushed her again. She just smiled at him.

"Or I could've just been reassuring her that it was all over between us," she added. "Maybe that's what I said."

He shoved her once more, harder this time, so hard that she fell against the wall. Her eyes glittered with excitement.

Jesus! She was enjoying it! It was just another game to her.

"It gets easy, doesn't it?" she said, standing up straight and licking her lips. Like a stripper, she slowly opened her robe, revealing all of her incredible body, letting the robe slide silently to the floor.

For a brief instant he wanted to kill her. His hands balled into fists. He wanted to hit her so hard, she'd—

He didn't hit her. Again, almost as if in a spell, he was overwhelmed by emotions he didn't understand. Frightening sensations, in that he had no control over them whatsoever. He was helpless, like a small fly caught in the enormous web of a hungry spider.

She was pure evil. His intellect knew that. Understood it well, in fact. She was probably a killer. Maybe a killer many times over. Who knew?

She was a consummate liar, a vixen, a sorceress. If he had an ounce of sense, he would be turning away from her, running for his very life, putting as much distance between them as possible. And forever.

That's what his intellect was telling him. But his intellect was overpowered by a base need, one kept well-hidden by the layers of reason that had encapsulated his brain.

Until he'd met this disturbing woman. Now the base need, the pure animal within him, crushed all intelligence, blew away the carefully layered reason, and reduced everything in life to one simple, mindless essential.

He didn't turn away. He moved to her, his body pressing against her nakedness. Slowly her fingers worked at the buttons of his shirt as she backed toward the bed.

Without a word he took off his clothes, a man in complete surrender. Brain dead, for all intents and purposes. A man with a heart and soul, and arms and legs and hands and feet and—

All of it useless, for the brain within was not functioning.

Rebecca stretched out on the bed before him, lying languidly, her body inviting, her breasts heaving, her nipples taut, her mouth open, her lips red and wet.

He lay beside her, fondling her breasts, then kissing them, running his tongue over her nipples. As before, he was a slave to her power, the smell of her as intoxicating as the strongest narcotic, the feel of her skin producing pleasure unlike any he'd known.

He brought his head down and plucked at her pubic hair with his teeth. Then he yanked hard. Rebecca moaned as she spread her legs and lifted her pelvis, pushing her vagina into his mouth.

His tongue darted into her wetness, exploring, licking, while his hand reached up and cupped her breast. She took his hand away and placed a finger in her mouth, sucking first one, then another. Then she closed her teeth on his thumb.

He jerked his hand away.

He felt her leg wind around him. Suddenly she made a move and ended up on top of him, her legs holding him fast. He felt cold metal against his arm. He jerked it away, and saw the handcuffs in her hands. His eyes grew larger.

"Are those the ones you used on Andrew?" he asked angrily.

She smiled knowingly. "Search warrants don't find everything."

Quickly he reached up and grabbed her, trying to flip her over. She struggled with the strength of a man, fighting for dominance. They were both sweating now, their skins slippery, their breath coming in short bursts from the effort.

He was too strong for her. Her strength was fueled by passion and excitement, but his was fueled by a combination of rage and the certain knowledge that he'd totally fucked up his life.

He had her pinned to the bed. His face was inches from hers, his eyes blazing with hostility, flecks of foam at the corners of his mouth, his cheeks flushed from exertion and fury. He held the handcuffs.

"Let's try something *new,* Rebecca," he hissed.

Using every ounce of his strength, he pinned her arm against the headboard and snapped a cuff on one wrist, the sound of metal against metal echoing in the room.

She grunted and kicked at him, missing by inches.

He was beginning to enjoy it. He seized the other wrist harshly, jerked it back, and pulled the handcuffs through the wrought iron. Then he snapped them shut over the other wrist. Again, she tried to kick him.

He laughed at her. "I thought you liked *everything*," he said viciously.

He had her. She was cuffed securely to the headboard. She twisted and turned, fighting to get free, but it was useless. He moved on top of her, spreading her legs with his knees.

Then he entered her roughly, his hands stroking her writhing, sweating body. His weight kept her pinned. She could barely move. He lowered his head to her breast, took the nipple in his mouth and bit down hard.

She screamed.

Suddenly, she sank her teeth into his neck. He bellowed in pain, then jerked back. He could see his blood on her lips.

Again, he laughed.

She was helpless now. He was the master. And she hated it. He could see it in her eyes. This *was* new to her, a complete reversal of fortune. And the terror blotted out the excitement.

"Are we having fun yet?" he asked.

"Fuck you!" she snarled.

"Good idea," he said.

He grabbed a breast and squeezed it hard. She groaned. Again, she bucked, trying to escape, but there was no escape.

He drove himself into her hard, his hands lifting her to him so the penetration would be at maximum.

They were both out of control. Insane. The rage bubbled within him, like a volcano ready to explode.

Again, he thrust deeply. She started to say something, but he jammed his arm across her throat.

"I . . . can't . . . breathe," she gasped.

He released his arm just enough to allow her to breathe, then continued as before, still grinding with his hips, kneading her flesh roughly with his hands.

He wanted to hurt her, wanted her to feel the pain. He wanted to kill her.

He wanted to fuck her to death.


He slept on a couch in his office. Biggs woke him up when the investigator arrived first in the morning.

The morning sun was streaming in the window, illuminating a thin layer of dust that had settled on the desk during the night, a desk clear of papers, for they were all scattered over the floor.

Biggs was shocked by Frank's appearance. Frank looked like a man who'd been on a weeklong drunk. But Biggs knew better than to ask any questions. Frank was always a little weird in the middle of a big trial.

"Hey, Frank!" he called.

Frank awoke groggily, rolled over, and slowly opened his eyes. His head pounded and his body ached.

For a moment he didn't know where he was, but as consciousness returned he recognized Biggs, sat up, and tried to shake the cobwebs from his mind. His mouth tasted like acid, and his stomach growled from hunger.

He rubbed his face with his hands and looked at Biggs. "Give me a minute, will you?"

"Sure, but I got something."

Frank waved a hand. "Wait till my brain is in gear."

Biggs left him alone.

Frank stood up, felt dizzy, then sat down again. He closed his eyes. The pounding in his temples increased twofold. He felt sick.

Memories returned. Horrible, disjointed

scenes. He and Rebecca clawing at each other, their bodies slapping together like animals, all pretense gone, all civility abandoned, just two pigs rutting in the pen.

She'd reduced him to a primary beast, a nothing. He wanted to cry.

He fought back a sob as he realized he could have killed her last night. He'd wanted to. He knew that much. And it could have happened if things had developed differently.

Jesus. He was a mess.

Sharon's face swam before his eyes. He saw her pointing at him in the alley, her face a mask of betrayal and hurt, telling him to get out and never come back.

He saw Rebecca laughing at him, taunting him, taking off her robe and thrusting out her breasts, daring him not to want her.

He'd folded like a cheap tent.

He slapped his forehead. Lights flashed behind his eyes.

He tried to stand up again. This time he made it. He walked slowly to the bathroom.

Like many trial lawyers, Frank kept a fresh set of clothes at the office. There was no shower, but there was a bathroom equipped with towels, soap, and toothpaste, even a razor.

Frank filled the sink with cold water, then stuck his head in the sink. The water spilled over and splashed over his shoes. He didn't care. The cold water was like a tonic, bringing him partly back to life.

He reached inside the medicine cabinet, found the aspirin bottle, and took three. Then he drained the sink and filled it with hot water, as hot as he could stand.

After ten minutes in the bathroom, Frank emerged looking almost fresh, but the puffiness under his bloodshot eyes advertised a tough night.

He walked into the conference room where Biggs waited, drumming his fingers on the mahogany table. "So, what has you so excited?" Frank asked. "You get something on Roston?"

"Sorry, but no."

"No?"

"No. There's nothing on the guy. I used a couple of friends, and the three of us talked to people all night. Roston was bitchin' about Rebecca to lots of folks. If he's lyin', he's been tellin' the same story for a long time."

Frank made a face. "Terrific."

"But," Biggs said quickly, "the night was not a total waste. I have something better than Roston."

"What?"

"You remember the Marsh tape?"

"Yeah."

"Well," he said, having difficulty containing himself, "Marsh was really into recording this shit. He could've opened his own video store."

Biggs picked up the remote control from the table and pressed a button. A video already cued in the machine began to play.

It was Marsh with Rebecca, with her on top, her favorite position. Rebecca was smiling at the camera. The voices were slightly garbled, but understandable.

"Move that . . . move that sweet ass," Marsh was saying.

"Like that?" Rebecca said, grinding.

"Oh . . . yeah," Marsh was saying.

"You forgot to say please," she said.

Frank closed his eyes for a moment. It was too much. He was fighting to erase his own memories of Rebecca, but there she was, doing what she did best, grinding and grinding and bucking and—

He had to watch. This was business. This was all that remained of his life, his work.

Rebecca threw her head back and thrust her breasts forward, then ground her hips into Marsh as she caressed her breasts and pinched her hard nipples. Then, slowly, her head came forward and her lustful eyes opened wide. She smiled at Marsh.

Frank watched her shift her weight, pulling Marsh with her, still locked inside her. She exposed his flank, then slapped it hard. Marsh moaned with pleasure.

Frank wanted to vomit. He'd seen this tape a score of times and it had had little effect other than to make him curious about what it would really be like to be in Marsh's place.

Now that his curiosity had been satisfied and the rot within himself revealed, watching the tape was pure torture. It awakened both his desire and his shame.

"How does this help us?" he said, wanting it to be over.

Suddenly the screen turned to snow.

"Keep watching," Biggs said, his voice betraying his excitement. "I would've missed it too, but the phone rang and I let the tape play while I talked. Garrett figured it was the end of the show. This isn't blank tape now, it's been erased."

Biggs's eyes were shining. "Just not quite all of it."

Frank waited.

An image appeared on the screen. The camera had been moved. It was no longer on a tripod, but being held in someone's hand. It tilted up a woman's naked body.

Not Rebecca, but another woman, a woman whose hands were shyly hiding her crotch.

Frank heard the woman's voice. She was giggling as she said, "Andrew?"

Frank thought he recognized the voice, but he turned to a grinning Biggs for confirmation.

"Uh-huh," the investigator said, beaming with pride at having discovered important evidence.

Frank turned back to the television. Marsh's excited voice could be heard clearly. "Move your hands, baby," he was saying. "Show me."

Joanne Braslow did as she was told, coy at first, then, as she got used to the idea, she began vamping. The camcorder focused on her breasts, then her face. Marsh was playing with the zoom, and the image expanded and contracted jerkily as Joanne started to do a dance for him.

Then the screen turned to snow again.

Frank was stunned. He sat there rubbing his mouth as Biggs shut off the machines.

"This was in his artsy phase before he went back to using a tripod," Biggs said.

Frank nodded. "She said they had a 'professional relationship.' Some profession."

"It gets better," Biggs said.

Frank grinned. "I don't know if I can *take* better, Charlie."

"Guess who was mentioned in Marsh's *prior* will, to the tune of a quarter-million sweet ones?"

"Joanne Braslow."

Biggs's face fell. He wanted to be the one to tell Frank, but the lawyer had figured it out. "Yeah."

Frank stood up and planted a noisy, wet kiss on the investigator's cheek.

"You're embarrassing me, man."

But he was pleased. Frank knew he was pleased.

He'd cracked it. Broken it wide open. The evidence had been there all along, just waiting for someone to see it. Garrett had missed it, as had the cops. For months, they'd all been scratching like chickens in a cage, looking for morsels of evidence to strengthen their side, and they'd all missed it.

But not Biggs. It might have been an accident, a fluke, but it didn't matter. What mattered was that he'd found it. And Frank was grateful.

"You know what you've done?" he said to Biggs.

"I think so. I think this is gonna help a lot."

He was grinning.

Frank shook his head. "More than that," he said. "You've saved my ass, Charlie. You've saved my worthless ass."

◆They were back in court. Rebecca sat next to Frank, her face a mask. When she'd greeted him in the parking garage, it had been as if nothing had happened. She'd smiled, said hello, and waited for him to enter the elevator.

She'd looked up at him, her eyes expressing the same admiration they'd held before. He was her lawyer and he was going to save her. That was all. Nothing had transpired between them. It was simply a fantasy.

He couldn't bring himself to speak to her, but he'd reconciled himself to her power. The inner conflict was gone.

Judge Burnham swept into the courtroom, took her seat, and the gathered assembly took theirs. Rebecca sat quietly, looking confident, a wisp of a smile on her lips, her hair arranged in a halo around her innocent head.

She wore a bright blue dress with a square neck, and three strands of pearls. As always, elegant.

Garrett stood up, full of himself, reeking with confidence. With a slight nod to the jury, he turned to the judge and said, "Your Honor, the state rests."

Judge Burnham looked over at Frank. "Is the defense ready to proceed?"

Frank rose to his feet. "We are, Your Honor. May we approach?"

The judge beckoned. With Garrett standing beside him, Frank made the obligatory motion asking for a dismissal of all charges. He knew his motion wouldn't be granted, but to fail to make the motion was a dereliction of duty.

Judge Burnham, as expected, refused to grant the motion, then told both lawyers to step back.

As soon as Frank reached his table, she said, "Mr. Dulaney, call your first witness."

Frank nodded. "Your Honor, the defense calls Dr. Raymond Wong to the stand."

Dr. Wong was called, took the oath, and settled comfortably in the witness chair. He looked at Rebecca, smiled, and nodded his head in recognition. Rebecca smiled back.

Frank led the man through some testimony to establish his credibility, especially that relating to the appellation of doctor, then asked him how long he'd been treating Rebecca.

"I've been treating Miss Carlson for over a year."

Frank stood near the witness chair, his arms crossed over his chest. "For what condition, Dr. Wong?"

"She suffers from painful menstrual cramps."

"And how have you been treating her?"

"I prescribed Chinese peony root."

Frank turned and saw the puzzlement in Garrett's eyes. Good. The bastard was in for a shock.

Addressing his witness again, Frank asked, "What does Chinese peony root *look* like, Dr. Wong?"

"It's a white powder."

The spectators, allowed back in the courtroom this day, mumbled softly. Frank stole another look at Garrett. Nothing there, but his plain-faced assistant was making furious notes, a pained expression on her face.

"How is this powder packaged?" Frank asked.

"It comes in a small bottle."

"A vial?"

"Yes."

"How do you instruct your patients to take it?"

Dr. Wong glanced at Rebecca again. "It's inhaled and absorbed by the mucous membranes."

Frank paused a moment, letting this information sink in, then said, "Thank you, Doctor."

He turned to Garrett, a thin smile on his lips. "Your witness."

But Garrett wasn't looking at Frank. His head was down as he studied some notes. "No questions," he said flatly.

Judge Burnham turned to Dr. Wong and said, "Step down, Doctor. You're excused." Then, to Frank: "Next witness, counselor?"

"Yes, Your Honor. The defense wishes to recall Joanne Braslow, but before we do, may I approach the bench?"

"Approach."

He couldn't help himself. He threw the confused Garrett a smile that would have melted a glacier in seconds. The jurors caught the exchange.

Together, the two men stood in front of Judge Burnham. Frank said, "Your Honor, the defense wishes to present an exhibit that requires a ruling. I would like to ask that this evidence be viewed in chambers."

"Very well."

"I'd also like to request that my associate be present. This may take some explanation."

The judge's eyebrows shot up. Garrett said, "What about my assistant?"

"Why not?" Frank said casually.

The judge turned to the jury and said, "I'll be seeing both counsel in chambers, along with their associates. Court is *not* in recess, so everyone just stay put."

She stood up and swept toward her chambers. Frank, Gabe, Garrett, and his assistant all followed. The spectators, unaware of what was happening, started buzzing, speculating.

In chambers, Frank asked for, and received, permission to play the Marsh tape. Garrett seemed perplexed, but raised no objection.

As the tape played, Frank watched everyone's faces. It was difficult not to look smug. The judge's face was expressionless, even when Joanne appeared on the screen.

Not Garrett. When he realized it was Joanne, his eyes bugged out of his head and his mouth fell open. He came partway out of his chair, a study in agony, his cheeks flushed, his forehead pinched in consternation.

His case was tumbling down around his ears.

Joanne Braslow, the professional, the caring, prissy secretary, was cavorting naked in front of his very eyes. She'd been making it with Marsh as well.

If this was murder, she had motive, opportunity, and probably the means. It was simply devastating.

Garrett sank back in his chair.

When the tape ended, Frank shut off the machine and looked at the judge.

She was quick and to the point. "I'll allow it," she said.

They all trooped back into the courtroom. Rebecca smiled at Frank, knowing from the look on his face that whatever had gone on was in her favor.

Garrett was trying hard to suppress his bitter disappointment, but it wasn't working. The gaze of the jurors, not privy to these secret goings-on, fell on Frank, then Garrett, then Frank again.

The room was charged with anticipation.

In a loud, clear voice, Frank said, "The defense wishes to recall Joanne Braslow to the stand."

Joanne's name was called and she walked to the witness stand from her seat at the back of the room. Again, there was a soft buzz of conversation. One look from the judge and it died down.

"You're still under oath," the judge said to Joanne as she took her place.

"Yes, Your Honor."

Frank gave Joanne a little smile. She was wearing makeup for the first time, at least so one would notice. And her dress was a little less conservative. All in all, she looked much different from the first time she'd appeared on the stand.

"Miss Braslow," Frank asked, "how much did you stand to inherit before Mr. Marsh modified his will in Rebecca's favor?"

Joanne's gaze dropped to her hands. "Two hundred fifty thousand dollars."

"And according to his final will?"

"Ten thousand dollars, which is still a large amount, and I'm grateful to him for remembering me at all."

Frank could hardly keep from laughing. She was lying through her teeth.

"After all your years of service," he said softly, "it doesn't seem like a lot."

"I'm not greedy."

The smile on Frank's face was gone. Now he wore another expression, the look a boxer has when he's about to deliver a knockout punch. They call it the killer instinct.

"No," he said sarcastically, "you're a saint. He cut you out of his will, he dumped you for a younger woman—"

Joanne, her face pale, said, "You're trying to make it sound like—"

Frank didn't let her finish. "And you can *still* find kind things to say about the man!" he bellowed.

Garrett raised a hand. "Objection. Counsel's arguing with the witness. Move to strike, Your Honor."

"I'll sustain it, and strike counsel's remarks," Judge Burnham said.

Frank had expected no less, but he'd said what needed to be said. She was a liar.

"Joanne," he instructed, "you have to start telling the truth now. Weren't you, in fact, a very personal friend of Andrew Marsh?"

"What does that mean?" she asked, her hands trembling slightly.

Frank's eyebrows arched. "Weren't you in fact lovers?"

"No!" she shouted.

Frank sighed, but it was for the benefit of the jury. He wanted to appear sympathetic in their eyes, a man destroying a person's testimony only because that person was lying. Just doing his job, and with some reluctance at that.

He turned and stole a glance at Rebecca. She was beaming, fairly bursting with confidence. Her enemy, a vicious woman bent on destroying her for selfish reasons, was about to be found out.

To Joanne, Frank said, "Do I have to enter into evidence the videotape Andrew made of you that indicates how very close you were?"

Joanne looked as if she'd been struck. "Oh, God," she blurted.

Frank waited.

Joanne struggled to compose herself, then said, "We dated."

Frank nodded. "Until he met Rebecca?"

She hesitated, then said, "Yes."

Frank nodded again, looked at the floor for a moment, then asked in a soft voice, "Did you still love him?"

"Of course I did."

"Didn't you think it was cruel of him to confide in you about Rebecca after he'd broken up with you?"

Garrett leaped up. "Objection! The testimony has no relevance to the issues in this trial."

"I'll withdraw the question," Frank said.

He took a step forward. "Were you hurt?" he asked Joanne.

"Same objection," Garrett bellowed. "Lack of relevance."

Frank was beginning to get steamed. Garrett had seen the tape in chambers. He knew what was coming, what the real truth was, and he was trying to obfuscate it. A bullshit move.

Frank moved toward the judge's bench. "Your Honor, this is a hostile witness. I'm trying to establish the depth of that hostility inasmuch as it may have colored her observations."

"Objection overruled."

Garrett was so upset his tongue started clucking involuntarily. The judge heard it and hissed, "Don't cluck at me, Mr. Garrett. This isn't a henhouse."

At the defense table, Rebecca was sitting with her hands in her lap, looking strangely demure. In an effort to avoid her adoring stare, Frank looked at the gallery, trying to gauge their reaction to what had just been heard. It was then that he spotted Sharon, several rows back, watching him. A shiver went down his spine. He avoided her eyes.

Frank turned back to face Joanne, but his train of thought had been derailed. Seeing Sharon had brought back a flood of emotions, the strongest of which was guilt.

He just stood there, saying nothing.

Finally Judge Burnham said, "Pick up the pace, counselor. I'd like to finish this trial before mandatory retirement sets in."

Rebecca, aware of Frank's moods, turned around and stared into the gallery. She immediately spotted the source of his discomfort and smiled sweetly at Sharon. Sharon glared back at her.

Frank fought hard to collect himself. He said, "Joanne, were you wounded by Andrew Marsh's intimate confessions to you about the woman who replaced you in his affections?"

Tears started running down the woman's cheeks. "What do you think? I was crushed. But I knew it wasn't going to last."

"And you expected Andrew to come back to you when it was over."

"Men don't marry women like that."

Frank gave her a look. "Didn't he tell you he'd *asked* Rebecca to marry him?"

She used her hands to wipe at the tears and succeeded only in making a complete mess of her makeup. Now, she looked grotesque.

"She turned him down," she said. "She already had everything she wanted from him."

"But *you* didn't," Frank said.

"Objection," Garrett cried. "Counsel's putting the witness on trial."

"She should be," Frank yelled.

Joanne protested. "I loved him! I would never have hurt him."

Frank was leaning toward her, his jaw thrust out, his arms held stiffly at his sides. Then he waved an arm as he said, "Even if he asked?"

"That's enough, Mr. Dulaney," the judge said. "An objection has been made and I am sustaining that objection. Strike Mr. Dulaney's question."

The judge leaned forward. "Was that your entire bag of tricks, counselor, or do you have another line of questioning with which to proceed?"

"I do, Your Honor."

"Then I suggest you get to it."

"Yes, Your Honor."

Frank addressed Joanne. "You testified that you ran personal errands for Andrew Marsh."

She was fighting to hold back the tears. "Yes."

The judge leaned toward Joanne and asked, "Do you need to take a break, Miss Braslow?"

Joanne shook her head. "Thank you."

Rebecca glowed. Clearly she relished what she was seeing, the collapse of the holier-than-thou Joanne Braslow, drug user, sexpot, hypocrite.

"Such as going to the drugstore for him?" Frank asked.

"Yes."

"Buying nasal spray for him because he had a cold?"

Her eyes widened. She knew where Frank was heading and it scared her. Frank turned away, took a file from Gabe, then stood in front of her again.

"You signed a house charge for the nasal spray on April eighth, the date of Andrew Marsh's death," he said.

Her mouth was opening and closing, but no words would come out. Frank bored in. "I'd like to introduce the receipt from Montclair Pharmacy as Exhibit"— he had to stop and look at his notes—"H. That was the bottle used to kill him. There was no other nasal spray found in the house. Isn't it true that *you* put in the cocaine?"

"No!" she shouted.

"Because you were jealous? Because he cut you out of the will? Because you have—"

Garrett was on his feet screaming objection, but Frank kept at it. "Because you have a cocaine habit to feed!"

Judge Burnham was yelling at Frank. "You're out of line, counselor! Objection sustained."

Joanne, shattered, looked up at the judge and, in a small voice, said, "I don't . . . I don't want to answer any more questions without a lawyer."

Frank turned away from her. He wanted to see Sharon's reaction. He was showing that Rebecca *wasn't* the killer after all, that he *hadn't* been made a fool. He wanted to see the look on Sharon's face.

He was to be disappointed. Her seat was now occupied by someone else.

"Permission to approach," Frank said.

Judge Burnham waved the two lawyers forward.

"In view of the testimony of the last witness," Frank said, "I'd like to renew my motion for dismissal of all charges, Your Honor. It's clear that the witness had motive and opportunity to murder Andrew Marsh, so much so that reasonable doubt as it relates to my client has been firmly established."

The judge looked at Garrett. "Not so, Your Honor," the assistant DA said. "There's no evidence to suggest that Joanne Braslow is responsible for this crime. She—"

"The nasal spray," Frank hissed. "She bought the—"

Judge Burnham cut them both off with one word. "Quiet," she bellowed. Then, sotto voce, she said, "I'm not about to bring these proceedings to a halt at this late date. I'll let the jury decide on all the evidence. Let's cut this short. Forget the motion, Frank."

"I'd like it on the record, Your Honor."

She glared at him. "Very well. Step back."

The attorneys returned to their tables.

Rebecca leaned forward and whispered, "You're doing a wonderful job, Frank."

He ignored her. He made his motion in front of the jury, for the record. It was immediately denied.

"As we have again reached the four o'clock hour," the judge said, "court is adjourned until tomorrow morning."

She slammed her gavel and left the room.

Frank leaned back in his chair, exhausted, but feeling pretty good. He'd expected his motion to be denied. That didn't alter the fact that reasonable doubt was building fast. Maybe not in his own mind or that of the jurors, but he'd established some reasonable doubt in the purely legal sense—

enough to pave the way for a possible appellate court reversal should the jury bring in a conviction.

That was part of his job.

Rebecca was right. He *was* doing a wonderful job.

"Five *years* together," Rebecca exclaimed, shaking her head. "She was never his type."

Frank and Rebecca were in the elevator that took them to the parking garage. The vision of a very shaky Joanne leaving the witness chair in tears, fully possessed of the knowledge that she was now a suspect in the murder of Andrew Marsh, stayed with Frank. He felt a little sorry for Joanne.

But the vision fled when they got off the elevator and entered the garage. Frank noticed that the smashed lighting fixture had been fixed. His gaze swept the area as he remembered, and a chill went down his spine. His temporary elation vanished as remorse cloaked him in a blanket of gloom.

"You sound jealous," he said to Rebecca.

Rebecca gave him a sharp look. "She killed him! She set me up to take the fall, and she almost got away with it. I don't feel sorry for her."

Frank tore his gaze away from the cars parked against the wall, pushing the disturbing vision of himself and Rebecca out of his consciousness.

Visions. His mind was full of them, whether he was awake or asleep. There was no escape. Again, he felt disoriented and adrift.

Frowning, he turned to Rebecca. "You know what bothers me? Why would she charge a three-buck nose spray that could be traced back to her if she planned to kill him with it?"

"Let *Bob* figure that out," Rebecca said.

"Maybe it was a crime of opportunity," Frank continued. "Maybe she's just stupid."

Rebecca stopped walking and looked up at him. "You mean maybe *I* did it."

"Maybe you did," he said matter-of-factly.

She was getting angry. "If the evidence hasn't convinced *you,* how the hell is it supposed to convince a jury? Do you ever look at their faces? They can't *wait* to convict me."

"All they need is reasonable doubt," he said.

"I know how their minds work," she said, still whining. "The women hate me, they think I'm a whore. And the men see a cold, heartless bitch they can pay back for every chick that's ever blown them off in a bar."

He stared deep into her eyes. "You could have helped change that perception. I almost begged you to dress more conservatively, but you refused. You said they'd have to take you as you were, that you weren't putting on an act for anyone. So don't complain about their perceptions, Rebecca. You helped establish them. Besides, I think you've got an inflated opinion of yourself."

Her eyes became cold. She looked at him as if he were a piece of trash. Then she said, "I have to testify."

"No."

"They're going to convict me if I don't. I need to tell my side."

Frank took a deep breath, exhaled, then said, "The only reason I'd ever put a client on the stand is if the case turned into such a disaster there wasn't any choice."

Rebecca was insistent. She jabbed a finger at him. "The difference is your clients are usually guilty," she shouted. "You told me that yourself."

"No," he corrected, his voice calm and confident, "I said they usually *did* it. Which is different than guilty as charged. Rebecca, I'm simply not going to let you fuck up my case."

"Jeff Roston fucked it up!" she shouted, her voice reverberating through the garage.

"Nothing's perfect," he said calmly.

She was beside herself. Hands on her hips, she looked around the garage, then exhaled some air. She took a different approach. The anger quickly dissipated. Now she looked like a misunderstood child.

"You owe me a chance to explain," she said softly.

Frank took another deep breath, exhaled, then said, "I'm listening."

He sat in his car parked by the guardrail, looking back at the houseboat, listening to the clicking sound of his emergency flashers. Curtains fluttered in the bedroom window, the soft light of the room beckoning as before.

He wanted to be there with Rebecca. God help him, but he did. He knew it.

But this time the last vestiges of common sense and reason took hold, and he declined her invitation.

The cool, damp air had seeped into his muscles. He felt stiff and sore. He also felt drained, alone and adrift. He rolled up the window and turned the key in the ignition. And as he drove away he still felt that strong tug calling him back.

He drove to the karate school. He arrived in time to see Sharon leave the school entrance with Michael. His wife had her arm over his son's shoulders and was walking him toward her car. For some reason, Michael turned around and saw Frank parking by the curb. He let out a yelp and came running to his father.

Frank was out of the car, his arms outstretched, and Michael flung himself into them. It felt incredibly good to have his son in his arms again. It had only been a couple of days, but he'd missed Michael terribly. The days seemed like years.

He held his son for a moment, then took him under the arms and swung him in small circles, much to Michael's delight. Then, another hug.

Looking over Michael's shoulder, Frank could see Sharon watching them. He gave her a loving look. He'd missed her, too. More than he thought possible.

His old life was shattered, gone. Now he was enmeshed in a new life, a frightening, strange world where the woman with whom he was involved controlled him like a puppet on a string. And as much as he despised this new life, he was unable to walk away from it.

Michael whispered into his ear, "She misses you."

Frank squeezed him one more time, then let him slither back to the ground. Michael gave him a look and then, with the wisdom of Solomon, took off to talk with his friends.

Frank hung his head as Sharon drew near. "I'm sorry," he said softly. "I'm so goddamn sorry."

"I'm not sure that's good enough," she said evenly.

It wasn't nearly good enough, he knew. But what else could he say? Could he confide in her? Tell her what it was like? Tell her about Rebecca's bizarre hold over him?

Could he tell her he'd never see Rebecca again?

Of course not. He couldn't tell her because he didn't know himself. His will was gone, his very soul now owned by a woman he could never trust completely. All he knew was that he wanted her. How the hell was he supposed to explain that?

At the same time, seeing the pain in Sharon's face was like a knife in the heart.

He turned away. He saw Michael and

Michael's friend Joey, both boys staring at Frank and Sharon. There was no mystery as to what was going through Michael's mind.

"At least they're talking," Michael said to Joey.

Joey, always the wise guy, replied, "That usually makes it worse."

Michael's face hardened. "You're not always right, Joey. Look! They're holding hands."

Frank had reached for Sharon's hand. She let him hold it for a moment, then slowly pulled it away.

Michael kicked at the ground.

"What are *you* getting mad about?" Joey asked.

Michael fought back tears as he said, "They're going to work it out."

"Don't hold your breath."

Michael looked at his friend, said, "Shut up!", gave him a shove, then ran back to his parents.

Frank fell asleep, fully clothed, on the office couch again, forgetting to close the curtains. This time the early-morning sun streaming in the office window woke him at seven. He sat up. Instantly his back screamed in protest. The couch was softer than the mattress he used at home, and the lack of support was taking its toll.

One of the secretaries had taken Frank's clothes and had them cleaned, so a fresh shirt, suit, and clean socks and underwear were neatly arranged in the bathroom closet. He said a silent thank you for the anonymous thoughtfulness, then stripped, and used the sink to give himself a bath of sorts.

A shave, a shampoo and rinse, and he felt almost clean. At least on the outside. He hung the wet towels on hooks to let them dry, placed his wrinkled suit and dirty clothes in a plastic bag, then dressed in fresh clothes.

He thought about Sharon. He remembered the look in her eyes as they'd talked. She'd been hurt so bad he doubted they'd ever get back together. He felt terrible about that, worse still that there wasn't anything he could say to alleviate her pain.

He wanted to cry.

He found the coffee machine and made a full pot. There was a day-old bagel inside a paper sack, and he wolfed it down as he waited for the coffee to filter through. Then, with a cup of steaming coffee in his hand, he went back to his office and sat at his desk.

The sun felt warm on his back as he made notes for today's appearance in court.

That was all that felt warm.

As was his custom, he reviewed his notes on the previous day's testimony, giving each response to a question a grade; plus one to ten points, or minus one to ten points. It was subjective, he knew, but it did help in determining how things were going. When he added up the score for the entire trial, he was thirteen points to the good. Not nearly enough.

But calling Rebecca to the stand might do the trick, especially after what she'd told him last night. Still, it was a terrible risk, for it left her open for cross-examination by Garrett. That could last an entire day, for Garrett wouldn't let a single response pass without attacking it from fourteen angles. Which meant Frank's examination would have to be short, cutting off Rebecca from hanging herself with her own words.

Rebecca was strong-willed, with a propensity for giving the finger to the establishment. Garrett knew this as well as Frank, and could easily goad her into making statements that would open a Pandora's box. Big trouble. Rebecca was quick to anger, and her innate hostility, combined with the impression already fixed in the minds of the jurors, could be very prejudicial.

But there was also the fact that despite their best intentions, jurors were leery of defendants who refused to take the stand on their own behalf. They liked to look into an accused's eyes as their innocence was proclaimed. They liked to make up their minds on the basis of eyeballing the defendant under pressure. It was human nature.

He looked at his notes again. Thirteen points to the good. An historically evil number.

Screw it. He'd told her he'd let her testify. He'd keep his word. It was her life. Perhaps there was some justice in having her future depend on her testimony. For that's where they were.

It was up to her.

He had just enough time left to grab a real breakfast before court. When he arrived inside the courtroom with Rebecca at his side, he looked for Sharon, but she wasn't there. His heart sank.

The clerk of the court intoned, "All rise!

The Superior Court for the County of Multnomah is now in session, the Honorable Judge Mabel Burnham presiding."

Judge Burnham entered the room and took her seat at the bench. She looked straight at Frank. "Call your next witness, Mr. Dulaney."

Frank was still standing. "The defense calls Rebecca Carlson, Your Honor."

Rebecca's chair scraped loudly as she pushed it away from the table.

Resplendent in a simple beige dress, she walked assuredly to the stand, stood before it, and took the oath.

"Do you solemnly swear to tell the truth, the whole truth, and nothing but the truth, so help you God?"

"I do," she said in a clear, slightly musical voice.

She then sat down, her head held high, her eyes focused on the jury. She smiled at them for a moment, then turned her attention to Frank.

The courtroom was as quiet as a tomb.

"Rebecca," Frank began, "I'd like to ask you to recount the events as you remember them on the night of April eighth."

A flicker of pain in her eyes. A catch of breath. Dripping sincerity. Jesus, she was good.

"We came back from dinner early," she said. "Andrew still had a cold, and I thought I'd just put him to bed and go home."

"But you didn't go home, did you."

She sagged a little. "No," she said, "He wanted to make love. And that made *me* want to. He was a very physical man."

"At sixty-three?"

She leaned forward, her lips almost touching the microphone. "He walked five miles a day," she said softly. "Even in the rain. That's how he caught his cold. He *wasn't* a weak old man."

"Would you say you loved him?"

"Very much," she said emotionally.

"Then why didn't you want to marry him?"

These were tough questions, he knew. He'd warned Rebecca that they would be accusatory. That way her answers would blunt Garrett's cross-examination. If Frank beat up his own client while she was on the stand, Garrett would appear as a brute, and the pendulum of sympathy would swing toward Rebecca.

"I didn't marry him because his marriages never lasted," she said, almost choking back a sob. Then she added, "I wanted to last."

Frank let that sink in, then said, "Rebecca, you heard the forensic testimony about the use of handcuffs."

Her eyes were downcast, embarrassed. "Yes."

"What were they doing in the house?"

As Frank asked the question he looked at Garrett. The man appeared to be mystified, for Frank seemed to be doing his job for him.

"Andrew bought them for Valentine's Day," she said, her voice timorous.

"For you to use on him while you made love?"

"Yes," she said softly. "Andrew liked that. He was always in charge . . . in his life, in his work. . . In bed, he liked to have somebody else in charge. It was a little game."

The spectators started laughing, some poking their friends in the ribs. They were enjoying this testimony immensely, having a great time.

Judge Burnham would have none of it. She cracked her gavel down and said, "Watch yourselves, or I'll clear the courtroom again."

They quieted down immediately. No one wanted to miss Rebecca's testimony.

"Rebecca, did Andrew indicate he was

having any problems at all, like shortness of breath, while you were making love that night?"

She shook her head slowly. "He was fine," she said. Then, looking wistful, she added, "He was happy."

"When you finished making love, what did you do?"

"I kissed him good night, and I went home. He was asleep when I left."

"When did you find out he was dead?"

Rebecca shuddered. She dabbed at her eyes with a white handkerchief, took a deep breath, then said, "Not until the next day. I felt like part of me had died."

Frank let that sink in as well. "And when did you find out you were the beneficiary of Andrew's will?"

"When you told me."

Frank looked at a still-perplexed Garrett, then turned back to Rebecca and said, "No further questions, Rebecca. Your witness."

But he stood there, not moving, still staring at her, suddenly afraid for her, terrified that Garrett would tear her apart. He wanted to protect her, save her from what might be coming.

The judge's angry words snapped him out of it. "Go sit *down*, Mr. Dulaney."

Frank's head jerked up. He looked at the

judge, then turned and took his seat. Garrett stood up, walked in front of his table, then sat on its edge.

"I'm less interested in your relationship with Andrew Marsh . . . the nature of which you've made abundantly clear . . . than I am in your relationships with Jeffrey Roston and Dr. Alan Paley. How long after you stopped dating Dr. Paley did you *start* dating his patient Mr. Marsh?"

She took the question well. "It must have been about four months."

"Four months in which you tried to *meet* your victim at galleries and museum openings?"

Frank was on his feet. "Objection. Counsel's baiting the witness."

"Not at all," Garrett protested. "I'm establishing premeditation."

"By baiting the witness?"

Judge Burnham waved her arm at both lawyers. "The objection is sustained."

But Rebecca couldn't wait for the next question. She had to explain, tell her side. "I never heard his name before I met him."

Frank tried and failed to catch her eye.

"You never saw his picture in the paper?" Garrett asked, his voice filled with incredulity.

"I don't read the paper."

"Is it your sworn testimony that by *coincidence* alone you happened to date both Andrew Marsh, who *died* from a combination of sex and drugs, and the doctor who treated him for drug poisoning?"

Rebecca gave him a slow smile. Jesus. Frank realized that this was just another *game* with her. It wasn't that she wanted to tell her side at all. She wanted to *play*.

The power games; sex was one, having her life on the line was another. It was all about control. Rebecca believed she could control anyone, including an experienced prosecutor with a sharp mind. She wanted to live on the edge—constantly.

"Portland's a small city," she said. "I even dated a man who dated a woman *you* dated. Like the old song."

Garrett flushed with sudden anger. "I don't know it," he said, his voice almost a snarl.

He saw her for what she was, and he didn't much like what he saw. He resented her snotty answers, her superior attitude, and her cavalier approach to convention. Most of all he resented her attempt to thwart justice.

She'd done Marsh in, all right. He knew it. But she was a clever bitch, manipulative and imaginative. Poor bastard Frank already looked like he didn't know his ass from page four. His client had obviously turned his brain into pabulum, probably fucked him senseless.

She wasn't going to make Robert Garrett look like a fool, not here in front of an assembly of reporters unlike any in Portland history. No way. Garrett raised a palm to the judge, who nodded.

Judge Burnham leaned toward Rebecca and said, "Do you think you're capable of just answering the questions put to you without all the chatter?"

Terrific, Frank thought. First he'd beaten up his client, then Garrett had gone after her. Now the judge was taking a few swings. Rebecca looked anything but sympathetic. She looked combative and arrogant. The jury was seeing her in a bad light. And when she spoke back to the judge by saying, "I'm on trial for murder, Your Honor. I'm trying to explain myself," Frank almost groaned aloud.

Frank looked at the jurors. He didn't like what he saw.

Perhaps the judge noticed the same thing. Rather than admonish Rebecca, she let the remark pass and motioned to Garrett. "Go ahead, Mr. Garrett."

Garrett nodded, took a moment, then

asked, "The night of Mr. Marsh's death, were you watching a pornographic video-tape you'd made of yourselves?"

"Objection as to characterization," Frank said, raising his arm.

Garrett didn't wait for the ruling. He rephrased. "An explicit videotape?"

A small smile played over Rebecca's lips. "Andrew used to say why watch strangers when you can watch friends."

One of the jurors laughed out loud, then quickly recovered. The judge glared at the jury box, then gestured to Garrett, who picked up a videotape box from his table and held it aloft.

"If you'd finished having sex and Mr. Marsh was asleep, as you've testified, then why was the VCR still on when the police arrived?"

"I forgot to turn it off before I left."

"Because Andrew Marsh was already *dead*? And you were in a hurry to make your exit?"

"Objection!" Frank bellowed. "Argumentative isn't the word for counsel's approach to cross."

"Sustained."

Garrett threw a hostile glance at Frank, then asked, "Miss Carlson, in your worldly travels, have you encountered cocaine?"

"Yes."

"You know how to obtain it, don't you?"

"I've never tried to," she answered.

"Answer the question!" he ordered, his face flushed with anger.

Rebecca's eyes flashed with fury. "I don't know how to obtain it in Portland, no!"

"Every high-school kid knows how," Garrett said derisively.

He was arguing with Rebecca again, barely able to contain his outrage. Frank objected, but before Judge Burnham could rule, Garrett almost screamed, "And you don't?"

"Asked and answered," Frank said.

Rebecca sat there smoldering.

The judge waved a hand at Garrett. "Move along, Mr. Garrett, you've made your point."

Frank was on his feet. "Your Honor, for the record, I'd like a ruling on my objection."

The judge glared at him. "For the record, your motion is sustained."

"I ask that counsel's remarks be stricken," Frank added quickly.

"So ordered."

The judge turned to the jury and said, "You will disregard Mr. Garrett's comment. It is argumentative and therefore improper.

The witness answered that she did not know how to obtain cocaine in Portland. That answer will stand."

Then, to Garrett, she said, "Move *along*, Mr. Garrett. You are trying my patience."

"Yes, Your Honor."

Frank sat down, repressing a smile. Rebecca took a deep breath, girding herself.

Garrett, red-faced, asked, "Miss Carlson, you stated that you handcuffed Andrew Marsh before you had sex with him the night of his death—"

"It wasn't before, it was during," she said matter-of-factly.

Garrett's eyes bulged. "Correction," he snapped. "Thank you."

He looked like he wanted to strangle her. She was getting under his skin.

"Did you engage in other forms of dominance with the victim? Did you, for example, beat him?"

Frank didn't bother to rise to make his objection. "The specifics of the relationship between the victim and the defendant have no bearing on the charges against her," he stated.

Garrett responded, "The state has an obvious interest in a pattern of abuse that ended with the death of the victim."

Judge Burnham turned to Rebecca and

said, "Answer the question, Miss Carlson. Succinctly, please."

Rebecca nodded, then said, "I never hurt him."

"Did you humiliate him?"

"No! I didn't humiliate him. He picked the games."

"Isn't that what husbands who beat their wives say?"

He was being argumentative again, and Frank objected without rising. He could see that Judge Burnham was getting upset, and when she beckoned both attorneys to come forward, he fully expected her to give Garrett a tongue-lashing. He wasn't disappointed.

As they both stood in front of the bench, she glared at Garrett and said, "I didn't impanel the jury for a course in sex education. If your cross-examination of the defendant consists of the entire Masters and Johnson index, cut it short."

Both lawyers returned to their positions. Garrett, fuming inside, was not to be denied. He wanted to destroy this woman's story, and he was going to succeed if it took six days, judge or no judge. Rebecca was a vicious, conniving, heartless killer, and he wanted to see her behind bars.

"You have a weakness for rich older

men with bad hearts, don't you, Miss Carlson?" he said.

She thrust out her jaw and replied, "I like self-confident men who aren't afraid to experiment. They tend to be older. And the people I meet tend to have money. I don't ask for profit-and-loss statements."

It was a haughty answer, the wrong thing to say at the wrong time. She was starting to appear hard and cold, even calculating. Her ego had taken hold, fueling her desire to show Garrett up in front of everyone. She didn't realize what effect her attitude was having on the jury.

But Frank did. He slumped in his chair. He couldn't help her now. This is what she had wanted. She was on her own.

"Rich older men with bad hearts who write you into their wills," Garrett continued.

Frank caught the judge's eye and made the obligatory objection. "Argumentative," he said.

"Sustained."

Garrett was determined. A thousand sustained objections wouldn't stop him. He had the look in his eye. The killer instinct.

"Are we supposed to believe that Jeffrey Roston is another coincidence, Miss Carlson?" he asked scornfully.

"They had nothing to do with each other," she said.

"Well, they both had bad hearts, didn't they? And they both wrote you into their wills."

Rebecca glanced at Frank, who was slumped in his chair. The expression on her face seemed to be trying to tell him to relax. She knew what she was doing. Then, to Garrett, she said, "I already testified that I didn't know about Andrew's heart."

"But you knew about Roston's heart."

"Yes."

"And when you couldn't induce a heart attack before he had surgery to *repair* it, you bailed out! He wasn't any good to you. Isn't that right?"

Rebecca hesitated. She dabbed at her eyes again, then slumped back in the chair as if the air had been let out of her balloon. In a small voice she said, "I left him when I found him in bed with someone else."

Garrett was unimpressed, but the jury seemed to take note. They sat up straight in their chairs, and the expressions on their faces softened.

"And that was grounds for walking out? As sexually liberated as you are?" Garrett said, his voice thick with sarcasm.

"I couldn't compete," Rebecca said softly.

Garrett was almost sneering. "You couldn't compete? Really. What was she *possibly* doing, was she using a razor blade?"

And then she hit him with it. Summoning up all of her remaining dignity, she leaned forward, her eyes misting slightly, and said, "He was in bed with another man."

The spectators, mindful of the judge's warning, whispered. Garrett stood there with his mouth open. Frank did as well. It was a masterful performance. A triumph. Had he spent six months coaching her, she could never have done it better. He was in awe of her talent. And she wasn't finished. Calmly, with great bearing, she said, "I never knew that about him. I felt . . . betrayed. I couldn't . . . handle it. I felt so rejected. And I left him. That was the right choice for both of us."

Garrett was ready to burst. "Mr. Roston isn't here to defend himself! You could say anything you want about him."

Rebecca remained calm. "It was easier for him to think I left because of the money. But I left because I couldn't stay."

She looked at Frank with an expression that pierced the wall of hate he'd developed. She seemed vulnerable again, a misunderstood woman, with strengths and weaknesses, and her own kind of dignity. Not the kind of dignity most people would understand, for it was the dignity of all people who found themselves scorned because of their beliefs, their handicaps, skin color, whatever. Different people, people who didn't flow with the main current. People who were, in the final analysis, oppressed, one way or another.

She was one of those, he believed. He also believed she was telling the truth.

Garrett gave up. She was too much for him. He was wary of making her appear even more sympathetic.

"No more questions," he said, his body sagging, the fight gone from him.

"Redirect, Mr. Dulaney?"

Frank stood up. There was no way he could improve on this turn of events. He smiled at Rebecca and said, "Your Honor, the defense rests."

"Very well," the judge said. "We'll hear closing arguments tomorrow."

She banged her gavel. The herd of reporters stampeded to the phones and uplinks.

The room erupted in sound. As the jury filed out, half of them looked at Rebecca, their faces reflecting their sympathy. The spectators were talking loudly among themselves, speculating.

Garrett pushed back his chair, slammed files into his briefcase, and stormed out of the room, his face flushed with undisguised rage.

Frank looked at Rebecca, now supremely confident, checking her makeup in a small compact mirror.

"That was quite a performance," he said.

She smiled at him. "You were wonderful," she said.

He felt that shiver in his spine again.

◆Biggs finally mentioned it. Frank saw him bringing a freshly cleaned suit and a package of laundry into the now deserted office, walking on his tiptoes, trying hard not to be seen as he placed the clothes in the bathroom closet.

Frank got up from his desk and went after him.

"So," he said as he entered the bathroom, "you're my guardian angel."

Biggs shrugged. "You need a little help, man. You've got things on your mind besides gettin' laundry done."

Frank leaned against the wall. "I really appreciate it, Charlie."

"No big deal, but if you're gonna sleep here all the time, you might think about changing the couch for a roll-away bed. You're lookin' a little more bent every mornin'. You keep sleepin' on that couch and it'll ruin your spine. You'll slip a disk or something. A man needs a good mattress more'n almost anything else."

Frank laughed. "So, that's the secret of life? A good mattress?"

Biggs's face got serious. "That and the love of a good woman," he said. "A man without at least one of those is in a load of trouble."

Frank's face fell.

Biggs was embarrassed. "Hey, I'm sorry, man. It's none of my business."

Frank shrugged. "It's not exactly the world's best-kept secret."

"True enough."

"You had dinner yet?"

"No."

"Care to join me?"

The big teeth gleamed.


They ate at Digger O'Dells in the historic barber-block area. Both ordered rare-cooked steaks, then nursed a beer as they waited for the food.

"I really fucked up, Charlie."

"I don't need to know, man. Really."

Frank sighed. "I'm talking to you because I know it'll never go further. Unless it makes you uncomfortable."

Biggs said nothing.

"It does, doesn't it?"

The investigator lowered his gaze and said, "I already know what happened. It's what I do, man."

Frank's eyebrows rose. "You saw us?"

Charlie laughed. "I didn't mean it that way. I saw nothing. It's just that it's written all over your face. Okay, I can dig it. The woman is something else, and there's no use trying to deny it. And you aren't the kind of man who can keep a secret from your wife for long. It just isn't your style. So I figure Sharon found out and threw your ass out on the street."

He leaned forward. "But hear this. Don't you be givin' up, man. Don't you go thinkin' this is the end. You give your marriage the same kind of attention you give your clients and you'll fix this thing."

Slowly a smile reached Frank's lips. "You're a clever bastard."

Charlie laughed again. "Hey, investigators have to be observers, you know? Gotta be able to read faces, tell when people are lyin', when they got stuff on their minds. Your face is like a road map. It doesn't take a genius to see it."

"I would say that's true."

"And knowing you," Biggs added, "if

you don't eat your food and get back to workin' on that closing statement, you'll be up all night. That's not too good either. You don't look so hot when you haven't slept."

"Thanks."

"Am I lyin'?"

"No."

"Okay. Why don't you sleep in a hotel tonight, get some real sleep?"

Frank grinned. "How many kids do you have?"

"Six."

"That explains it."

They both laughed.


Frank took the advice, and in the morning he felt refreshed. He took his first real shower in days, shampooed and blow-dried his hair, and brushed his teeth until they gleamed.

His blue pinstripe suit was cleaned and pressed, and a new white shirt purchased by Biggs fit perfectly. With the red power tie firmly in place and his shoes freshly polished, Frank was ready for court.

While he felt confident about the case, the guilt gnawed at him constantly, fighting for his attention. The tremor in his hand was constant now, and he found himself sticking the hand in his pocket so no one would notice it. Unrelenting stress always took a physical as well as mental toll.

His eyes were more pinched than normal, and slight pouches had formed beneath them. He seemed to have aged five years in a matter of days, a result of the interminable conflict raging within him.

His self-esteem as a lawyer was still high, but as a man, he felt near worthless, and when he was alone, he could see it reflected in his expression. He made a pledge to himself to be vigilant. The jury must never see him like this.

When he sat next to Rebecca at the defense table, it was with a different attitude. While he'd always contended that she was innocent, at least to others, he now firmly believed it, and his entire demeanor reflected this heartfelt belief. Whatever had gone on between them was personal. It had nothing to do with this trial. He owed her his complete dedication, and he was determined to pay that debt.

Rebecca looked frightened, and Frank's heart went out to her. While she was still dressed strikingly, her hair and makeup perfect, her eyes expressed the same fear and uncertainy they'd shown when he'd bailed her out of jail five months ago.

It seemed like years ago. So much had happened.

Even though Rebecca's testimony of the previous day had been tremendously helpful, Frank could tell that her confidence was ebbing. She'd played the game to the hilt, seemingly enjoying every minute. But now it appeared she was unsure if she'd won.

With closing arguments the last item on the agenda, the case would be in the hands of the jury. They would determine her fate. He could almost see the wheels turning in her head. Had they believed her? Did they think she was a whore? Worse yet, did they think she had killed Andrew Marsh? That was the only important question.

Frank touched her hand. "We'll win this, Rebecca," he said softly.

She put on a brave smile. "I have confidence in you, Frank."

Behind them, the spectators chattered, edgy, awaiting the call to order. Reporters were already making furious notes, and there was the sound of people nervously sitting in their seats, tapping their feet or drumming their fingers. And always talking. The buzz of their incessant conversation echoed in the room.

Finally the clerk of the court rose to his feet and intoned, "All rise!"

The chatter stopped, replaced by the sound of rustling clothes and scraping of chairs as everyone stood.

One of the spectators had a scarf pulled tight over her head, dark sunglasses covering her eyes. But those close to her recognized her as Joanne Braslow.

Two benches away, Sharon Dulaney stood quietly, then, as Judge Burnham took her place behind the bench, she sat down, her eyes riveted on her husband.

Frank, his attention focused on the notes he'd placed in front of him, noticed neither woman.

Everyone was seated and the noise evaporated. Now absolute quiet reigned.

"You may proceed, Mr. Dulaney," the judge said.

Frank stood up. "Thank you, Your Honor."

He walked slowly and stood in front of the jury box, feeling alive with fresh energy. The tingle in the pit of his stomach was back, a good sign.

"Ladies and gentlemen," he began, "the prosecution's case is built on sand. Where are the facts? Where's the evidence? What links Rebecca Carlson to the death of Andrew Marsh other than the prosecutor's wishful thinking?"

He threw his hands in the air as he answered his own question. "Not a damn thing."

He shook his head as he said, "The only thing he's been able to establish beyond a reasonable doubt is that the defendant and the victim both liked unconventional sex."

He smiled at the jurors. "That's not a crime in the state of Oregon."

He waited for a moment, then said, "But Mr. Garrett would like you to think that if Rebecca could wander off the well-worn paths of accepted sexual behavior, then she must be a murderer!"

Again, he shook his head. The movements were designed to impart the feeling that Garrett was confused, misled, totally off the mark.

Frank looked at each juror in turn. Then he said, "Rebecca Carlson didn't force Andrew Marsh to make love to her. He was grateful for the chance!"

He swung around to face Rebecca.

"Look at her!"

He pointed to Rebecca. She had her hands folded in her lap, her face expressing a calmness that belied the turmoil raging within her.

Her soft, blond hair hung down almost to her shoulders, vibrantly accentuated by the blue of her dress. Her dark eyes were focused on the jury, and she looked at each and every one in turn, just as Frank had instructed.

She seemed bathed in serenity, as if broadcasting the message to the jurors that she was quite willing to place her very life in their capable hands.

"It's human nature," Frank said, dropping his arm. "We want what we want . . . when we want it. Desire can hit like a freight train. We do things without thinking about the consequences. The future doesn't exist!"

His words rang true, his own experience gilding each one in a layer of solid gold.

"Andrew Marsh didn't tell Rebecca about his heart disease because he didn't want to lose her," he continued. "It was his life and his choice. And finally his mistake. He was . . . consumed by passion, like a fire inside him. He let it burn. . . ."

He took a deep breath, exhaled, then said, "Andrew Marsh knew his own risks. He died doing exactly what he wanted."

He turned away from the very attentive jury, took two steps, then faced them again.

"During your deliberations," he said, "please remember the two most important words in the American legal system . . . reasonable doubt. I know you'll do your duty and find Rebecca Carlson . . . not guilty."

As he walked back to his table he spotted Sharon sitting among the spectators. She was smiling at him, a sort of wry, congratulatory smile. He felt his heart skip a beat and a feeling of hope flooded his body.

The look of hate was gone from her eyes. Did that mean she was ready to forgive him?

He wanted desperately to believe that it did.

Now it was Garrett's turn. The prosecutor stood up slowly, buttoned the jacket of his blue suit, and walked to the front of the jury box.

He started by thanking the jurors for their careful attention during the trial. He buttered them up good, telling them how dedicated and responsibly they'd acted throughout.

Then, his voice dripping with sincerity, he said, "Andrew Marsh was seduced and murdered by a woman who thought she could make it look like a natural death."

As Frank had done, he shook his head sadly. "Well, she was wrong. Sex and drugs are not a natural death, ladies and gentlemen! Not when the intention is murder."

He took a deep breath, exhaled, and

said, "And Rebecca Carlson had every intention of inducing a fatal heart attack. She had ten *million* dollars at stake."

He let that sink in for a moment.

Then, his voice rising in intensity and volume, he said, "She knew Andrew Marsh had a hypersensitivity to cocaine. She dated the doctor who treated him for it! All she had to do was taint the nasal spray and then apply her extensive sexual skills."

His hand stabbed the air like a knife. "Andrew Marsh didn't stand a chance. The day he made Rebecca Carlson his sole beneficiary, he signed his own death warrant."

Again, Garrett shook his head slowly, crossed his arms across his chest, and paced in front of the jury box. He was playing the room for all it was worth.

Then he let his arms drop to his sides and faced the American flag, one of two that flanked the bench. Slowly he brought his arm up and pointed to the flag. "But I believe in our system of justice."

He turned and faced the jury. "And I respect twelve reasonable men and women. I know that based on the evidence in this case, ladies and gentlemen, there is no reasonable doubt about the guilt of the defendant."

His hands gripped the railing surrounding the jury box. "And when you come back into this courtroom with your verdict of guilty," he said passionately, "you'll be telling Rebecca Carlson, 'No, you *can't* get away with murder. Murder must be punished.'"

His voice as soft as velvet, he finished by saying, "Murder *will* be punished. I'm confident of that."

He took his seat. Once again, there were murmurs among the spectators.

Judge Burnham's instructions to the jury were short and sweet. She reminded them of the law, told them they must not allow personal biases to interfere in their judgment, that they must weigh only the evidence and the testimony, and that to find Rebecca Carlson guilty, there must be a total absence of reasonable doubt.

"Reasonable doubt," she added, "means just that. It suggests that you, as jurors, are reasonable, thinking people. And so you are, or you wouldn't be sitting where you are.

"When you weigh the evidence, you must be convinced *beyond* all reasonable doubt that the defendant is guilty if you are to return that verdict.

"If, on the other hand, you *find* reasonable doubt, you must find the defendant not guilty."

Then, after some short additional comments, she sent them away to consider a verdict.

With a bang of the gavel, she left the rest of the room to wait and wonder.

The babble of voices resumed, but no one left the courtroom.

Frank felt Rebecca's hand on his. "What do we do now?" she asked.

"We wait."

"Here?"

"Absolutely. At least for the first couple of hours. It usually takes them a while to figure out how they're going to handle the voting. If we don't hear after a couple of hours, we can go to an interview room or my office, if you prefer. We have to be no further than ten minutes away."

"How long do you think it will take them to decide about me?"

Frank shrugged. "It's impossible to say. It could be as little as an hour, or as long as days. We might even get a hung jury."

Her eyes were imploring. "And?"

He made a face. "Then we get to repeat this entire trial."

Rebecca sighed in exasperation. "You saw their faces. You were right up close to them. What do you think?"

Frank smiled weakly. "I gave up trying to read minds a long time ago. You'll just have to hang in, Rebecca."

"You're not much comfort," she said sharply. Then: "I have to pee."

Sharon Dulaney was standing in front of the big mirror in the ladies' room, staring at her reflection with a critical eye. She saw some new lines, the ravages of days and nights of crying and worrying. Mostly sleepless nights, lying alone in the big bed, reaching out in her sleep for a man who wasn't there, a man who'd betrayed her.

She fought back a tear as she pushed the thoughts from her mind. She applied some moisturizer to her face, then started to reapply her makeup. She was putting on her lipstick when she heard a toilet flush and saw Rebecca emerge from one of the stalls.

Rebecca stood beside her, washing her hands, looking at Sharon in the mirror. She took some paper towels and wiped her hands. Then she played with her hair a little and opened her handbag.

"Wish me luck," she said cheerfully.

Sharon slapped her so hard, Rebecca

bounced off the sink, almost losing her balance.

Sharon stood there, her face flushed, her hands formed in fists, ready to strike again.

Rebecca's clothes were expensive, but beneath them was nothing but a cheap whore. A sick, depraved, greedy killer. That was bad enough. But this bitch had tried to ruin Sharon's marriage by seducing her husband. And she knew why. Rebecca didn't want Frank. She didn't give a damn about Frank. All she wanted was a lawyer who lusted after her, a man who would do almost anything to save her from jail so he could screw her at his convenience.

Well, Sharon wasn't giving up without a fight. If Frank managed to save Rebecca's well-worn ass, she'd have Sharon to deal with.

Sharon waited, but Rebecca made no effort to strike back, so Sharon turned on her heel and strode out of the rest room without another word.

Rebecca watched her leave, faced the mirror, rubbed her cheek, then smiled broadly. Her eyes were shining with excitement.

She calmly removed a small silver compact from her handbag and started applying powder to the red imprint left by Sharon's blow.

The jury took just three hours to reach a verdict. When the word went out, everyone poured back into the courtroom where the main participants remained: Garrett, his assistant, Frank, Gabe, and Rebecca.

Garrett and Frank exchanged glances. Garrett wore a smile, but Frank was impassive. He knew Garrett was just as unsure, that the smile was for the benefit of the women in the room. Garrett always played to the women.

Rebecca's eyes were wide with fear. She gripped Frank's arm. He wanted to pull away, but didn't. She was still his client and this was the moment of truth.

They watched as the jury filed silently back into the box. Frank noticed three men and one woman looking at Rebecca, a good sign. But there were eight jurors who avoided looking at her, a bad sign. None of them smiled. Another bad sign.

And they'd been quick. Too quick for a hung jury. The tingle in his stomach became a dull ache.

The judge was addressing them. "Ladies

and gentlemen of the jury, in the case of the *People* versus *Rebecca Carlson*, do you have a verdict?"

The foreman rose to his feet. "We do, Your Honor."

He passed the verdict slip to the bailiff, who carried it to Judge Burnham. She read it without expression, then gave it back. The bailiff then took it to the clerk of the court.

Rebecca was about to jump out of her skin. Gabe patted her on the hand and she threw him a look of gratitude. Frank rubbed a temple. He could hardly bear the tension.

"The jury," the clerk intoned, "finds the defendant . . . not guilty."

The gallery exploded in shouts, some praising the verdict, others expressing disgust. Reporters started to make a mad dash for telephones, but the banging gavel stopped them.

"Quiet!" Judge Burnham shouted.

Frank felt the tension drain from his body, leaving him slightly dizzy. Behind him, Gabe hugged Rebecca.

The judge, expressionless, said, "The court thanks the jury. The defendant is released from bond, is free to go, and this court is adjourned."

A smash of her gavel, and the rush of activity resumed. Joanne Braslow walked stiffly out of the courtroom, jostled by some of the ruder reporters in a hurry.

It was over.

Frank sat down, feeling slightly faint, his head swimming with emotion.

He'd done it. He'd saved her.

He rubbed his eyes. Then, as he remembered, he got shakily to his feet, his eyes looking to the departing spectators.

"I told you," Rebecca called to Frank.

He didn't respond. He was searching for Sharon.

He saw her by the door, looking back at him. Waiting for him. His heart leaped.

He started to walk away. Rebecca pulled at his sleeve, caught up to him, then whispered in his ear. "Thanks, Frank. You almost convinced *me*."

It was as if the earth had stopped spinning on its axis. Everything stopped; sounds, movements, his heart. Total isolation. His entire being was focused on a pair of eyes, the eyes of a cunning woman who belonged in hell.

He was speechless. He knew he wasn't breathing. The woman from hell was grinning at him like the Cheshire cat. Then she turned and sauntered down the aisle, threw

Sharon a glance, and walked out of the room to the waiting forest of cameras and microphones.

He stood there, waiting for the earth to start moving again.

Jesus. She'd done it. She'd killed the poor bastard, taken on the system, and beaten it, giving a performance worthy of the greatest actor in the world. And she'd done it her way, thumbing her nose at convention, at society, at everyone, including Frank.

He felt dirty and ashamed. He felt duped. He felt stupid and worthless.

Slowly air entered his lungs, sounds assaulted his eardrums, and smells tickled his nostrils. His senses were returning.

All of them, especially the sense of shame.

He walked slowly down the aisle toward Sharon. Behind him, Gabe was almost skipping with happiness. Biggs held the associate back as Frank neared Sharon. Frank took his wife's arm, and together they left the courtroom.

In the corridor Rebecca was holding the assembled press in adoration. She was surrounded, but loving it this time. No more ducking the press. Now she was reveling in her victory, standing tall and straight, her chest thrust out, her head high, her eyes sparkling with excitement.

She was tossing off one-liners like a stand-up comic and they were laughing, lapping it all up like thirsty long-lost nomads. She was a star, basking in the bright glow of notoriety. But she saw it as celebrity.

Frank and Sharon walked past her, ignoring her. They were unnoticed. Frank took Sharon's hand in his. Their fingers laced.

"I didn't think you were going to be here," he said softly, his eyes beseeching.

"I've never missed a closing argument," she answered. "You were good."

His jaw tightened. "I was good enough."

As they waited for the elevator he bent over, took her in his arms, and kissed her. Her lips tasted sweet, and he wanted to cry.

He'd almost lost her. Michael, too. All because of his failure to see past the carefully manufactured facade that was Rebecca. But she'd seen through *his* facade and exploited it to the fullest.

He'd left his brains behind, letting his penis do his thinking. He'd succumbed to the oldest trick in the book, been ready to throw away everything he really wanted for a few moments of illicit pleasure with a woman who didn't care if he lived or died.

The woman now in his arms cared. Cared deeply. Always had. Now she was giving him a second chance.

He didn't deserve it, but he was grateful.

Reluctantly Sharon pulled away from his embrace and looked into his eyes, searching. "She's watching," she said.

"That's her problem," Frank replied sincerely.

The elevator arrived and Frank put her aboard. "I'll see you later at the coffeehouse," he said. "I have to sign some papers, get the bond returned—you know, legal stuff. I'll get there as soon as I can. I love you."

Still not sure of herself, Sharon looked troubled, but before she could respond, the elevator doors closed in her face.

Frank looked back at Rebecca. She was staring at him, that look of twisted admiration in her eyes.

He turned away. She was poison. Absolutely toxic. And he was allergic to her. He had to stay away from her no matter what. He knew that now.


Frank got the paperwork straightened out, then decided to take the stairs leading

from the courthouse to the street. The courthouse was almost deserted, the media army
gone, the excitement over until the next big
one. He wanted some air before heading to
the coffeehouse.

As he descended the stairs he saw movement behind a marble pillar and pulled
back. Someone was there. Someone he
couldn't see. But he knew the voice.

"You're a good lawyer," he heard Joanne
Braslow say.

Then she stepped out from behind the
pillar. Obviously she'd been waiting for
him.

She looked like death warmed over. Her
skin was ghostly pale, her eyes red from
crying, her makeup smeared, her hair
disheveled, even her clothes seemed askew.

She was also having trouble breathing.

"You know how to sell the biggest lies!"
she said bitterly. "And now they're going to
hang it on *me*. *I'm* the only suspect."

He held up a hand to stop her, but she
continued talking.

"She knew you'd see the tape," she said
heatedly. "She knew you'd find out I do
coke. I was perfect for her. That's why she
used coke to kill him, don't you see? She
was setting me up."

He knew she spoke the truth. Rebecca

had fooled a lot of people. But she hadn't fooled Joanne.

"Joanne," he said, trying to calm her down. She would have none of it.

She was closer now. "It *wasn't* peony root," she exclaimed. "That was pharmaceutical cocaine! Because I took it out of her purse and used it myself!"

Frank wanted to tell her he believed her, but he couldn't. He was a lawyer. There were rules.

"It was the best I ever had," Joanne continued, her face a mask of hate and anger. "I don't care if you believe me. But she committed murder and you helped her get away with it."

Suddenly she was spent, the anger gone. Now she was just humiliated and devastated. Her body sagged as her strength vanished.

He could understand.

She turned and stumbled away from him, crying, almost blinded by her tears. He reached out and placed a hand under her elbow.

"Here, I'll help you," he said.

And above him, fifteen steps away, Robert Garrett stood with his mouth agape, his eyes wide, his cheeks flushed with rage. As Frank and Joanne moved away Garrett swung a foot at a pillar, then jammed his hands in his pockets. It was all he could do to contain himself.

The stupid, stupid woman! Had Joanne told the truth from the start, they would have nailed Rebecca good. Damn! Why did they always lie?

The sun was just setting when Frank arrived at the dock. He parked the car by the guardrail and stepped into the cool evening air. He watched a forty-foot yacht as it moved majestically downriver, trailing a white-foamed wake. Above it, some birds screeched, then swooped toward the water in search of food.

He strode purposefully down the wooden slats leading to Rebecca's houseboat.

It had to be done. He had to find out the whole truth even if it meant seeing her again. What had happened between them was an aberration, a departure from the path he wanted his life to take. But he had learned from his mistakes. He would never risk losing Sharon again.

When he reached the door to her houseboat, he found it locked. He bent down and lifted the mat. Nothing. Then he tried the flowerpots. No key.

He walked around the side of the houseboat. The sliding glass door leading from the deck was open, the drawn curtains billowing in the gentle breeze coming down the black river. He pulled them back and stepped into the darkened room.

He could hear Rebecca in the kitchen amid the sound of clattering dishes. Then, as he moved closer, he could make out her words.

"It's better than the lottery," she was saying. "It's tax free."

Then he saw her, Little Miss Domesticity, moving in and out of his sight as she placed dishes in the cupboard. He heard a man's voice, but it was just a murmur, the man out of his field of vision.

"Oh, screw your *career,*" Rebecca said. "You just made a million dollars, baby! You knew you were going to blow your career."

She was coming toward Frank, her hands full of glasses to be placed in the bar. Stealthily he sat down in a chair.

"I'm doing you a favor," Rebecca said over her shoulder. "We'll live happily ever after! But not together. Because if you hang around me, you'll get yourself indicted for perjury and murder.

"I'm home free," she added. "They can't try *me* again. But you're a different story."

And then the man entered the darkened room. Even in the darkness, Frank knew it was Alan Paley.

"I love you!" Paley said, his voice pleading and filled with hurt. "I did it to *be* with you!"

Rebecca switched on a light. Immediately she saw Frank and jerked back. "Shit . . . Frank."

Paley also stopped in his tracks, his mouth hanging open.

Frank just sat there, a look of disgust on his face.

"He *heard* us?" Paley asked Rebecca.

Rebecca waved a hand. "He's my lawyer. It's privileged."

Frank's face now wore a mask of anger. "I'd have given you the same goddamn defense," he said bitterly.

Paley moaned, then said, "He's going to bury me."

Frank and Rebecca ignored him. They were glaring at each other, like pit bulls about to engage in mortal combat.

"You wouldn't have been as believable," she said, matter-of-factly.

Frank's eyebrows shot up. "If I didn't fuck you?"

She shrugged. "It works."

Paley looked aghast. He stared at Frank

and then at Rebecca, the dawn of comprehension tugging at the corners of his eyes.

"What?" he mumbled. "Did you . . . you slept with him?"

Rebecca smiled, still facing Frank. She was full of triumph, queen of the world, conqueror of any who stood in her way. Her consummate arrogance filled her with contempt for those with the temerity to question her motives or methods. She knew best.

"I don't think we ever slept, did we?" she said to Frank, mocking the now disintegrating Paley.

Frank didn't respond.

Rebecca turned and faced the stricken Paley. She talked to him as one would talk to a moron.

"Oh, don't look so hurt, Alan," she said, her voice filled with ridicule. "I fucked you, I fucked Andrew, I fucked Frank. That's what I do. I fuck. And it made me ten million dollars. Well, nine anyway."

She sounded proud of her accomplishment.

"Poor Joanne," Frank said softly.

Rebecca grinned at him malevolently. "Every crime needs a suspect," she said.

"So," Frank said, "you're fucking Dr. Paley here, and he mentions a rich patient. You figure you can screw yourself into the will . . . you know how to *do* that."

Rebecca started laughing. A hard, brittle, metallic little laugh. "I'm hard to resist," she said.

Paley was beside himself. He was confused, his face a tortured mask of conflict. "Why are you telling him?" he asked.

Rebecca corrected him. "He's telling *us*, baby."

Frank was indeed. He knew it all now. "The coke came from Dr. Paley, didn't it?"

"Made it untraceable," she said cheerfully.

Frank shook his head in grudging admiration. "Fuck if you didn't play me perfectly. Paley goes on the stand to make you look guilty as hell. Then you set me up to destroy him so I can make you look innocent."

He laughed derisively. "Sort of a reverse character witness. You're a real genius."

She was through playing games for the moment. Now she just wanted Frank out of her house.

"I can't say that about you," she hissed. "I always thought the message on the answering machine was a little over the top, but you even bought that."

So they'd even faked that, Frank thought. Clever. Again, he shook his head. He had to hand it to her.

"What are you doing here, Frank?" Rebecca asked. "Ambulance chasing? You looking for a new client? Talk to Alan. He thinks he's in trouble."

It was too much for Paley. He looked like a switch had gone off in his head. Suddenly it was all clear to him. All the sex, all the attention had been nothing more than part of her master plan. A way for her to get rich.

She'd been focused on her wants from the beginning, and Paley was just another piece of the puzzle, to be moved about as Rebecca saw fit.

He was nothing to her. Frank was nothing to her. Even Marsh had been nothing to her. She was incapable of love, more a machine, a greedy, scheming machine without a soul. And Paley had been stupid enough to have fallen in love with her, fallen in love with a designing, heartless, soulless fucking machine.

"You don't give a *shit* about me," Paley wailed, his eyes almost bugging out of his head.

She put her hands on her hips and gave Paley a look of pure contempt. "You're right," she said harshly. "I've already forgotten about you."

Paley's bugged-out eyes seemed to spin

in his head. The humiliation was utterly unbearable. Not only had he been made a total fool, but he was looking at possible prosecution. And if he read Rebecca right, there was a guarantee he'd be charged. She'd see to it, the bitch.

He wouldn't even see the money she'd promised. By the time all that paperwork was done, she'd have spilled her guts to the cops and Paley'd be sitting in prison. And no matter what he said, what truths he told, or how many people backed him up, they could never prosecute Rebecca again.

It was overwhelming. He finally cracked.

He grabbed a heavy glass ashtray from the table and swung it at her head, screaming, "You cunt!" as he swung.

She ducked. He missed her by inches.

"What is *wrong* with you?" she yelled.

The ashtray was still in Paley's hand. He was stalking her now, getting ready to try again. "I threw my life away for you," he said, his voice filled with wonderment, the awe of full discovery.

He started moving toward her, the arm holding the ashtray held high, ready to come crashing down on her skull. She scuttled backward, her eyes filled with terror.

"You're going to be a rich man," she said, as if not comprehending his anger.

He didn't care. As he lunged Frank seized his arm and held it fast.

"Drop it!" Frank commanded.

It was like Frank wasn't even there. Paley was still staring at Rebecca, a wild look in his eyes. "I don't give a fuck about the money."

Then he drove his elbow back into Frank's stomach. Frank loosened his grip. Paley was free. Rebecca charged toward the stairs, trying to escape.

Paley, his body propelled by rage, was on her in an instant, grabbing her foot and upending her. The coffee table fell over with a thud, some little crystal figurines tinkling as they smashed against the plush carpet.

Rebecca was pinned under the heavy table. Paley, wild-eyed, started stomping her viciously.

Frank grabbed him by the neck and tried to pull him away, but the enraged Paley was sweating profusely, and Frank's grasp slipped. Paley struggled free and wrapped his arms around Frank, pushing him backward. For a moment they moved back and forth as they struggled, each trying to get the upper hand.

Rebecca was screaming and Paley was cursing, and Frank was trying to get things calmed down.

The two men moved about the room, locked in each other's arms, knocking over lamps and furniture, kicking at each other, trying to break free.

A cacophony of sound reverberated throughout the room as lamps smashed to the floor and wood split in pieces, the sounds almost drowned out by Rebecca's screams and Paley's guttural curses.

Frank finally broke free and punched Paley hard in the stomach, but it didn't stop the man.

Paley's high adrenaline level was making him insensitive to pain. He lashed out with a foot, catching Frank on the shin. A spike of pain almost bent Frank over. He straightened up and aimed a punch at Paley's head.

It missed.

Then Paley caught Frank with a blow to the solar plexus that sent him reeling against the wall, gasping for air.

Rebecca finally wriggled free of the coffee table and bolted for the stairs. Paley saw her, lost his interest in Frank, and dived toward Rebecca, trying to grab her leg, but he missed. She scooted up the stairs like a squirrel, Paley hot on her trail.

Frank's mind was spinning. Jesus! He should have resisted the impulse to have one last confrontation with Rebecca. Every time he was with her, pain was involved. Now he was caught in the middle of a battle between two deranged conspirators.

Rebecca had sucked Paley in just as she'd conned Frank. Both men were just instruments to be used in her ferocious desire to be rich.

But she'd underestimated Paley. The man was ready to kill her, and she'd stoked his fires of hate by mocking him. Her incredible arrogance had overridden the brilliance that had conceived her successful plan.

Stupid, stupid people.

He had to get up there, to the bedroom. Now. His chest screaming in pain, he ran for the stairs.

In the bedroom, Rebecca headed directly for the bedside table. Paley knew what she was after, lunged toward her, managing to push her away, and yanked out the drawer. He came away with a gun in his hand and an insane gleam in his eyes.

Frank was there at last, his legs throbbing, his heart pounding, his lungs begging for air. He saw the gun and leaped toward Paley. The gun went off, the bullet grazing Rebecca's neck.

She screamed in pain. Blood ran from the wound onto her dress.

Frank now had Paley's gun arm in his grip, but Paley, consumed with rage, was as strong as a mule. The gun went off again, shattering an aquarium. Shards of glass, multicolored fish, and thirty gallons of water spilled onto the floor, making it as slippery as ice.

Paley wrenched his arm from Frank's grasp. His eyes jerking crazily, he brought the gun up. Frank lunged at him, sending him spinning across the floor. Paley's feet slipped on the wet carpet and he sailed down the stairs, head over heels, coming to a crashing heap at the bottom.

Frank, his entire body a mass of pain, peered down at the unmoving Paley. The gun was nowhere in sight. Frank turned away, gasping for air.

His arm ached unmercifully, and an eye was throbbing. There were various cuts on his face that stung like bee stings. His chest hurt, and his stomach heaved. He wanted to puke.

He took another look at Paley. The man looked unconscious.

Frank turned back to look at Rebecca. Dazed, she was struggling to get to her feet.

"Are you all right?" he asked.

"I think so," she said in a hoarse voice, "but you look like hell."

"I'll live," he said. "Come on, I'll help you."

He lifted her to her feet. She looked into his eyes and said, "Get me out of here, Frank." Her voice sounded weak.

He wanted to tell her what he'd come to tell her, but it was pointless. She'd never change. She'd never listen to him. She'd do what she wanted to do whenever she wanted to do it.

That was the real Rebecca. A killer, yes. A manipulative bitch, yes. Evil, certainly. Perhaps the embodiment of all that was evil.

But he couldn't leave her there and let Paley kill her. That wouldn't solve Frank's terrible dilemma.

"Okay," he said softly.

She was on her feet and starting to move when another shot rang out, the sound of it deafening. This one struck her square in the chest, sending her staggering backward, hitting the window, shattering it.

Frank turned instinctively. He saw Paley at the top of the stairs, his gun hand coming down slowly.

Jesus.

Frank turned back to Rebecca. The window had shattered completely and she was falling backward, almost as if in slow motion. He reached for her outstretched hand and missed.

Just as it had in the courtroom, when Rebecca'd told Frank she had killed Andrew Marsh, the world stopped spinning.

It was quiet and peaceful, and Rebecca was slowly floating out the window backward, her arms and legs extended, her blond hair floating in the breeze, the dark stain between her breasts growing rapidly.

She was looking at him. Not in fear, but in peace, as if she knew it was over. There was almost a smile on her lips, as if she understood this was the way it had to end. And her eyes stayed locked on his all the way down.

And then her body hit the river with a loud splash and sank out of sight.

The body floated back to the top a few seconds later, the eyes still open, lifeless now, the gentle ripples of water lapping at her open mouth, the water turning red where it touched her chest.

Frank turned back to Paley, sitting on the bed. The gun still dangled from his limp hand.

Paley knew what he'd just done. He knew his life was over as well. But it didn't matter. It was already over before he killed her.

"I loved her," he said sadly, as if that explained everything.

Frank took a pocket square from his jacket, inserted it into the trigger guard, and lifted the gun from Paley's unresisting hand.

"We both made a mistake," he said softly.

◆They were still crawling all over the houseboat—cops, crime-scene technicians, divers with scuba gear, just as they had all night.

On the other side of the yellow ribbons on the dock stood reporters, TV crews, more cops, the ME's van—and the simply curious.

The curious; the people who stood gawking at the aftermath of a terrible traffic accident, or a fire, or a street killing. They stood and looked for no apparent reason, staring at the blood and smashed bone and wrecked flesh, shaking their heads in dismay and mumbling to each other.

They were always there, and Frank never ceased to wonder why.

He was sitting on the deck of Rebecca's houseboat, his entire body aching from the terrible struggle with Paley, his face bandaged and swollen, one eye almost closed, an arm in a sling, the shot the paramedics had given him just starting to wear off.

He was oblivious to the light rain falling, wetting his hair, dampening the shoulders of his jacket.

Garrett sat on another chair across from him, not caring about the rain either, looking off into the night, then shaking his head.

"You could have waited, you know."

Frank grunted. "No. I wanted to give them the statement now, while it was still fresh."

"Do you believe in karma, Frank?" he asked.

"No."

The dampness finally started to get to him. Frank stood up on wobbly legs. They hurt. Jesus. Everything hurt. His body was swimming in pain.

"I'm going home," he said wearily. "It's been a hell of a long night."

Garrett stood up and moved out of the rain. "You're entitled."

"Thanks."

"About that karma. Whatever you call it, people usually get what they deserve . . . except for lawyers."

Frank gave him a look, then nodded. "Usually, but not always."

The two courtroom adversaries watched as the bag containing Rebecca's body was carried outside and placed on a waiting gurney.

"You should've won the case, Bob," Frank said softly.

Garrett shrugged. "I did," he said.

The gurney's wheels clattered noisily as the ME's people moved it beyond the yellow ribbon and down the dock. Frank limped slowly after it, pain shooting up from his ankle to his hip.

As he climbed the stairs to the street Frank looked up and saw a familiar figure walking toward him. Sharon looked so vulnerable in the early-morning light, he winced at the thought of the pain he had caused her. He held out his good arm to her and held her close, wishing he could erase the past few months.

"Are you all right?" she asked, her eyes filled with concern.

"I'll be okay," he said, brushing his lips against the top of her forehead.

"I'm so glad you called," she said.

"Me, too."

They took a few steps, then Frank noticed the sun starting to peek over the horizon. He stopped.

"What's the matter?" Sharon asked.

"Nothing. It's a new day."

He looked into her eyes. "Sharon, I'm so sorry. I realize how much I hurt you. I can't explain. I really can't. I just beg you to forgive me."

She placed her fingers on his lips to silence him.

"It's like you said, Frank. It's a new day."

He put his arm around her shoulder. Together they walked toward his car.

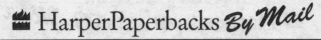

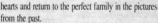

## PAINTED BLACK

Carl A. Raschke

Carl A. Raschke, America's leading authority on subcultures of darkness, documents an invisible wave of evil that holds America's children by their minds and parents by their hearts.

## PRIVILEGED INFORMATION

Tom Alibrandi and Frank H. Armani

The gripping story of an attorney who risked everything—including his life—to protect his client's horrifying secrets.

## VALHALLA'S WAKE

J. Loftus &
E. McIntyre

John McIntyre, a young Irish American falsely branded a spy, became the innocent victim of an incredible international conspiracy involving the IRA, CIA, KGB, British SAS, and the Mafia.